FROM THE NANCY DREW FILES

THE CASE: *A series of suspicious accidents and fires threaten to bring the curtain crashing down on Connecticut's Red Barn Theater.*

CONTACT: *Evelyn Caldwell has starred on Broadway and in the movies, but now she needs Nancy to take center stage.*

SUSPECTS: Joseph Brunner—*The playwright is locked into his contract with Evelyn . . . unless he can write the Red Barn out of the show.*

Fiona Sweeney—*The technical director has a secret reason for hating Brunner's play, and she'd love to see the whole production go up in smoke.*

Charles Ferguson—*The businessman lives next door to the Red Barn, and lately he's been putting the heat on Evelyn to sell the property.*

COMPLICATIONS: *Nancy is not only in pursuit of an arsonist, she also has to keep her eye on actress Laura James, who seems intent on building a fire between herself and Ned.*

Books in The Nancy Drew Files® Series

#1 SECRETS CAN KILL
#2 DEADLY INTENT
#3 MURDER ON ICE
#4 SMILE AND SAY MURDER
#5 HIT AND RUN HOLIDAY
#6 WHITE WATER TERROR
#7 DEADLY DOUBLES
#8 TWO POINTS TO MURDER
#9 FALSE MOVES
#10 BURIED SECRETS
#11 HEART OF DANGER
#12 FATAL RANSOM
#13 WINGS OF FEAR
#14 THIS SIDE OF EVIL
#15 TRIAL BY FIRE
#16 NEVER SAY DIE
#17 STAY TUNED FOR DANGER
#18 CIRCLE OF EVIL
#19 SISTERS IN CRIME
#20 VERY DEADLY YOURS
#21 RECIPE FOR MURDER
#22 FATAL ATTRACTION
#23 SINISTER PARADISE
#24 TILL DEATH DO US PART
#25 RICH AND DANGEROUS
#26 PLAYING WITH FIRE
#27 MOST LIKELY TO DIE
#28 THE BLACK WIDOW
#29 PURE POISON
#30 DEATH BY DESIGN
#31 TROUBLE IN TAHITI
#32 HIGH MARKS FOR MALICE
#33 DANGER IN DISGUISE
#34 VANISHING ACT
#35 BAD MEDICINE
#36 OVER THE EDGE
#37 LAST DANCE
#38 THE FINAL SCENE
#39 THE SUSPECT NEXT DOOR
#40 SHADOW OF A DOUBT
#41 SOMETHING TO HIDE
#42 THE WRONG CHEMISTRY
#43 FALSE IMPRESSIONS
#44 SCENT OF DANGER
#45 OUT OF BOUNDS
#46 WIN, PLACE OR DIE
#47 FLIRTING WITH DANGER
#48 A DATE WITH DECEPTION
#49 PORTRAIT IN CRIME
#50 DEEP SECRETS
#51 A MODEL CRIME
#52 DANGER FOR HIRE
#53 TRAIL OF LIES
#54 COLD AS ICE
#55 DON'T LOOK TWICE
#56 MAKE NO MISTAKE
#57 INTO THIN AIR
#58 HOT PURSUIT
#59 HIGH RISK
#60 POISON PEN
#61 SWEET REVENGE
#62 EASY MARKS
#63 MIXED SIGNALS
#64 THE WRONG TRACK
#65 FINAL NOTES
#66 TALL, DARK AND DEADLY
#67 NOBODY'S BUSINESS
#68 CROSSCURRENTS
#69 RUNNING SCARED
#70 CUTTING EDGE
#71 HOT TRACKS
#72 SWISS SECRETS
#73 RENDEZVOUS IN ROME
#74 GREEK ODYSSEY
#75 A TALENT FOR MURDER
#76 THE PERFECT PLOT
#77 DANGER ON PARADE
#78 UPDATE ON CRIME
#79 NO LAUGHING MATTER
#80 POWER OF SUGGESTION
#81 MAKING WAVES
#82 DANGEROUS RELATIONS
#83 DIAMOND DECEIT
#84 CHOOSING SIDES
#85 SEA OF SUSPICION
#86 LET'S TALK TERROR
#87 MOVING TARGET
#88 FALSE PRETENSES
#89 DESIGNS IN CRIME
#90 STAGE FRIGHT

Available from ARCHWAY Paperbacks

The Nancy Drew Files™

Case 90

Stage Fright

Carolyn Keene

AN ARCHWAY PAPERBACK
Published by POCKET BOOKS
New York London Toronto Sydney Tokyo Singapore

AN ARCHWAY PAPERBACK *Original*

An Archway Paperback published by
POCKET BOOKS, a division of Simon & Schuster Inc.
1230 Avenue of the Americas, New York, NY 10020

Produced by Mega-Books of New York, Inc.

ISBN: 0-671-79482-5

First Archway Paperback printing December 1993

10 9 8 7 6 5 4 3 2 1

Cover art by Tricia Zimic

Printed in the U.S.A.

IL 6+

Stage Fright

Chapter One

WHY WOULD ANYONE want to burn down a theater?" Nancy Drew asked, peering at the road through the sheets of water that slipped down over the windshield. Her rental car crept along the dark country road, its headlights cutting through the watery dusk, the wipers battling the downpour. "Arson makes me so angry when I think of all the innocent people who could get hurt!"

"Or even die," added Ned Nickerson, Nancy's boyfriend. He switched on the overhead light for a second to check the directions Nancy had scribbled down, then brushed his wavy brown hair back and squinted out the passenger-side window. "Looks like we're coming to Bridgeville. The theater is a few miles past the center of town."

Nancy glanced at the clock on the dashboard. "It's four-thirty. This thunderstorm has really delayed us."

"I sure wouldn't expect one in December," Nancy's friend, George Fayne, said, wiping the fog from the rear window. Her curly dark hair was tussled from the ski cap she had removed and tossed on the seat beside her. "Especially in Connecticut. If this were snow—"

A jagged streak of lightning followed instantly by a cannon shot of thunder stopped her in midsentence.

"Wow, that was close," Nancy said. "Seems like this storm has followed us all the way from the airport."

"I just hope lightning doesn't hit Aunt Evelyn's. She has enough problems," George said.

Nancy drove past a wide green with a statue of a Revolutionary War soldier in its center. The green was bordered by a white church with a towering steeple, a town hall, a library, and ten or twelve large, comfortable homes aglow with Christmas lights. "Don't worry, George, we'll find out who set the fire at your aunt's *and* who sent the threatening notes, too."

Ned put his hand on her shoulder and grinned. "If Nancy Drew can't do it, no one can."

"I just wish we had more time," Nancy said, shaking her head. "Opening night is Friday and it's already Tuesday. Ms. Caldwell will have to cancel the show if we don't move fast."

George leaned forward. "Dad said Aunt Evelyn can't afford to cancel the play."

Nancy had never actually met Evelyn Caldwell, but she knew of her, of course. She was a famous actress who'd starred in dozens of Broadway plays and Hollywood movies. She had retired from acting three years earlier to run a summer theater and try her hand at directing. She wasn't really George's aunt, just a close family friend. She and George's father had grown up together, and George was extremely fond of her.

Now Evelyn Caldwell was the owner and artistic director of the Red Barn Theater, a historic little New England playhouse. Under her the theater had gained a reputation for excellence, attracting top actors from New York City and audiences from all over the state. But the theater was expensive to run.

"I know about the financial problems," Nancy said. "She told me on the phone that when she decided to run the theater year-round this fall, the actual costs of adding insulation and a heating system turned out to be much higher than she'd been told."

"Plus, she's invested so much money in this play that it *has* to be a success," George said. "She's hired two stars and paid the playwright a fortune for the rights to the premiere of *Alias Angel Divine.*"

"But if she does have to cancel this production," Ned said, "can't she make it up with proceeds from the rest of the winter season?"

"Not if someone burns down the Red Barn." George threw herself back against the seat, frowning.

"Don't worry," Nancy said, reassuring her friend.

As they left the lights of Bridgeville behind, Nancy felt the surge of excitement that always accompanied the beginning of a new case. This time, for George's sake, she was doubly determined to find out who was behind the threats.

"Hey, Nancy," Ned said, "there's the sign."

As Nancy slowed the car, she caught sight of a big wooden Red Barn sign. She turned left and drove down a muddy lane with pond-size puddles. Following the directions Ms. Caldwell had given her, she went past the theater and some small buildings to turn right at a low, rambling building the actress called the Lodge. Next door was a white clapboard house. Nancy pulled up there.

"There's Aunt Evelyn's house!" George cried excitedly. "It's so quaint—just the way she described it."

"We'll have to make a dash for it," Ned said.

"Let's go." Nancy flipped the hood up on her

hot pink ski jacket, opened the car door, and ran for the shelter of the porch with her friends.

"We don't exactly look ready to meet a major star," Nancy said. A few damp ends of her shoulder-length reddish blond hair poked out from under her hood, and curly wisps were plastered to her forehead.

After George had rapped twice, Evelyn Caldwell opened the door. Nancy's first thought was that she was smaller in real life than she appeared on the movie screen. Then Nancy took in her gorgeous high cheekbones and wide-set eyes and understood why she had had such presence on screen. Although the actress was now in her forties, she was lovelier than ever.

"George, dear, how good to see you. It's been much too long." She ignored the wet jacket and gave George a big hug. "Come in out of this awful weather." She ushered them into a pine-paneled foyer. "You must be Nancy. How wonderful of you to come."

Nancy shook the slim hand she was offered. "We're happy to be here. This is my boyfriend, Ned Nickerson. He and George have helped me solve lots of cases."

"It's lovely to meet you," she said, smiling at Ned. "Why don't you hang your wet things on these pegs, then come in by the fire. I've made a pot of tea."

When Nancy entered the living room, she saw

a gaily decorated Christmas tree, holly wreaths at the windows, and a fire crackling on the hearth. It was the perfect set for a holiday scene. It was all perfect except for the tension Nancy sensed in the famous actress. Evelyn Caldwell's hands trembled slightly as she passed out teacups and carrot cake, and she kept rubbing her neck in an uneasy gesture.

She and George spent a few minutes catching up on family news, then Nancy put down her cup and took a notebook from her bag. "Would you mind filling us in on the problems you mentioned on the phone, Ms. Caldwell?"

"Oh, please call me Evelyn." She frowned. "Let's see—where to start. The first note appeared almost a week ago, but I didn't take it seriously. I thought it had to be a joke."

"What did it say?" Nancy asked.

"Exactly the same thing as the others that followed. I have them all here." Evelyn opened a drawer in the table beside her and handed Nancy several papers. "Someone sticks them in my script and I find them at the worst possible moments."

" 'When the curtain goes up, it will be in flames,' " Nancy read out loud. The notes were identical, with the same sentence typed in the middle of each sheet. Nancy recognized the tiny scraps left when the perforations on form-feed computer paper are carelessly removed. "This looks like a computer printout."

"Yes," Evelyn said. "And the typeface is the same as that on the computer printer we have in the office."

"Who has access to it?"

Evelyn sighed. "Everyone. The office is unlocked, and people are in and out all day."

"Who knows the word-processing program?"

"The entire crew. We're a small group and everyone pitches in to get the job done."

A tremendous clap of thunder shook the house after lightning lit up the room to artificial brightness. Rain streaked down the windows, closing in the living room to make it snug and warm. "Can you tell me who is here?" Nancy asked.

"Well, there are the actors, of course. We have only two, Matt Duncan and Laura James."

George almost dropped her cake. "Matt Duncan is here? *The* Matt Duncan?"

Evelyn nodded.

Pleasure—mixed with panic—washed over George's face. Nancy knew that her friend had a secret crush on Matt Duncan, who played Brent on their favorite soap opera, "Ventura Boulevard." It was so unlike George to fall for a TV star that she avoided discussing it, even with Nancy.

Evelyn continued, "Then there's Joseph Brunner, the playwright. I produced another of his plays last summer. He's very talented, but he's quite a character. I'm directing the play, so only those three are from outside."

"What about the staff?" Nancy asked.

"Emily is the cook, and her husband, Ed, is the groundskeeper. In the theater, Fiona Sweeney is technical director, and she's in charge of our six crew members and two apprentices."

"That's not very many," Nancy commented.

"No, but we manage," Evelyn replied. "They're the ones who make the theater go—they run the box office, build the sets, do the lights—you know, all the backstage work. They're really nice kids, and each one is invaluable."

Evelyn leaned back in her chair, as if exhausted. "That's the problem. I just can't imagine who'd want to harm the theater, or this production. Everyone stands to gain if the play and the Red Barn are a success."

Ned's damp wavy hair glistened in the firelight as he leaned forward. "So you're not sure if the threats are directed against you, the theater, or the play that's about to open?"

"That's right." Evelyn nodded. "But no matter what, everyone would lose. If the theater burns down, the staff would be out of jobs, and if the play doesn't open, the actors and the playwright will miss a chance to present a play I'm betting will be a hit when it moves to Broadway."

"You mentioned a fire that you discovered in the greenroom," Nancy said.

"Yes." Evelyn shuddered. "Fortunately, I happened to find it before it got out of control.

Someone had left a stack of paper cups on the hot plate while it was still on."

"Did you call the police?" Nancy asked.

"I didn't dare. They would have reported it to the fire marshal, and if he found out about the arson threats, he would close the theater down."

"Isn't that a little drastic?" Ned asked.

Evelyn shook her head. "You can't subject an audience to the chance of fire. Of course, the barn has been sprayed with fire retardant, but it won't hold up against a really hot blaze."

She rubbed the back of her neck again. "That's why I called you, Nancy. I can't afford to have the theater closed down. Yet I don't want to endanger the lives of my audience. I'm begging you to find out who's behind this before opening night. George says you're the best."

"I'll try," Nancy promised. "What precautions have you taken?"

"I've hired three security guards to work round-the-clock. They cost a fortune. This play *has* to pay off—a Broadway run, maybe movie rights. I've gambled everything I have on it."

"May I keep these?" Nancy indicated the anonymous notes and Evelyn nodded. "Who knows about these threats?"

"No one except the guards and my friend Marla Kramer, who's staying with me. I didn't want to worry the cast and crew."

"Marla Kramer," George said. "That's a familiar name."

"You've probably seen her on TV a hundred times. We've been friends for twenty-five years, since we were both young actresses in New York. She had no work commitments, so she's helping me turn the Barn into a year-round business. Until recently she had her own theater, out in California. She's a little forgetful, but she's a big help, especially with publicity."

"If the company doesn't know about the threats, how did you explain the security guards?" Nancy asked.

"I told everyone it was a new state law," Evelyn said, smiling wryly.

"And they believed it?" Ned was astonished.

"They're much too busy to worry about a detail like that. This show is a major undertaking." Evelyn turned to Nancy. "My first priority is to find out who's behind these arson threats, but at the same time, I don't want to jeopardize the play. That's why I've asked you to keep your work secret. I can't have the cast and crew upset."

"No problem," Nancy said. "Ned and I have tagged along with George to visit an old family friend for the Christmas season. Just a holiday get-together, right?"

Evelyn's answer was cut off by a flash of white light outside the windows and a tremendous crash of thunder.

"Some Christmas weather you're having." George grinned.

"I'll paraphrase Mark Twain. If you don't like the weather, just wait a minute," Evelyn said, forcing a smile. "It could be balmy tomorrow."

They all laughed, but then Evelyn grew serious again.

"I'm really trying to keep all this in perspective," she said. "But I am very worried. If I take a loss on this new play, I'll have to sell the Red Barn, probably to my new neighbor, Charles Ferguson. He's made an offer on the property through his attorneys."

Just then the front door crashed open and a tall, slender woman rushed in, bringing a blast of cold air with her.

She stopped when she saw Evelyn, her eyes wide with fright.

"Oh, Evelyn, hurry. There's a fire!" she said.

Evelyn gasped.

Nancy jumped up and ran to the window and her heart skipped a beat.

Near the rear of the Red Barn, vicious shafts of flame were shooting up into the night sky.

Chapter Two

NANCY AND THE OTHERS grabbed their coats and dashed out into the rain. The Barn wasn't on fire, luckily. A shed behind it was burning, lighting up the whole area with an orange glow.

"Oh, no, it's the prop shed!" Evelyn moaned.

As Nancy ran toward the small building, she saw that a group of people had already gathered. The shed must have been burning for a while before they were alerted, she thought.

The rain started to let up as Nancy and her friends arrived at the building. Two men in security guard uniforms were squirting hoses at the crackling building.

"Where are the fire extinguishers?" Nancy shouted.

"In the Barn!" a girl with long frizzy red hair said. "Come on!"

Nancy, Ned, and George followed the girl into the rear entrance of the theater, grabbed the cylinders, lugged them back to the shed, and sprayed foam over the blaze. The rain helped to douse the fire, and twenty minutes later the floodlights on the Barn revealed a steaming, smoky ruin, which included the blackened remains of five artificial Christmas trees.

"Well, the salesman guaranteed they were flameproof," the redhead said bitterly. "He didn't promise they'd stay green—or decorated."

"It took me *hours* to trim those trees," a stocky girl beside her protested.

"Do you know how many stores I went to to find dinner plates with a holly pattern?" a lanky guy groaned.

"Okay, guys." The redhead straightened her shoulders. "We haven't lost anything that can't be replaced. We'll find, make, or repair whatever we need." The redhead turned to the director. "Right, Evelyn?"

Evelyn had been silently staring at the ruins, but now she shook herself out of her daze. "Yes, of course. We'll manage, Fiona."

The rain had tapered off to a soft drizzle, and only a few wisps of smoke curled up from the charred remains. The group talked quietly, speculating about how the fire had started and how they were going to replace the lost items.

Fiona spoke sharply. "Okay, enough moaning and groaning. Let's get to work!"

"Yeah, sure," the lanky guy mumbled.

"Cut it out, Jerry!" Fiona shot back.

"Okay! Okay!" He held up his hands. "But can we eat first? It's past dinnertime."

Fiona glanced at her watch, then said in a controlled voice, "All right. Food, then work."

She started down the hill toward the Lodge, where everyone, cast and crew, ate and relaxed. After a few backward glances at the ruined shed, the crew trailed after her.

"Thank goodness for Fiona," Evelyn said weakly.

Nancy turned to Evelyn. The older woman was visibly shaken. "Fiona's the technical director, right?" Nancy asked gently.

"Yes, she's really something." The tall woman who had alerted them to the fire answered for Evelyn. She was very slender, with shimmering blond hair, and she spoke in a fluttery voice. "I'm Marla Kramer, Evelyn's friend, and *you* must be Nancy Drew, the *famous—"*

"Marla," Evelyn said in a low warning tone, nodding at a short, plump man standing nearby. He had black hair and dark, deep-set eyes only partly obscured by thick-lensed glasses. He was hugging himself to keep warm while he stared at the ruins. Without raising her voice, Evelyn made it carry. "Joseph, don't worry. We'll find a way to open the play on Friday, in spite of this."

"I don't see how," he said, thrusting his hands in his coat pockets. "I never should have allowed you to stage it. This wouldn't happen in New York."

Evelyn gave Nancy an ironic look. "Of *course* not. There are *never* fires in the Big Apple."

He scowled. "I think it was arson." His pitch rose on each word. Nancy could tell he was extremely high-strung. "How could lightning start a fire like this?" he went on. "Did you see how fast it spread? Someone is trying to destroy my play."

"Nonsense," Marla said briskly. "Why would anyone want to do that? You're just upset."

"I agree," George said, glancing at Nancy. "Who would try to set a fire in a downpour? It had to be lightning. Remember that big crash of thunder we heard before Ms. Kramer arrived?"

"Call me Marla, please." The tall woman put her arm around George's shoulder. "And you're George. I recognize you from Evelyn's photos. Let me have a *good* look at you." She fumbled in her pockets. "Now, *where* did I leave my glasses this time? Never mind, I can see you're *lovely*. And who is *this* handsome fellow?"

"This is Ned Nickerson, a friend of mine—and Nancy," George offered.

Marla continued to study Ned for a moment as she lit a cigarette. "*Gorgeous*. Have you ever considered acting, young man?"

Ned blushed, embarrassed by Marla's frank stare. "Uh, not really."

Evelyn tried to rescue him by introducing the short man, who turned out to be the playwright, Joseph Brunner.

"Nice to meet you, Joe," Ned said pleasantly.

Brunner seemed to grow six inches as he pulled himself up. *"Not* Joe. *Joseph."*

"Oh, sorry, um, Joseph." Ned was even more embarrassed.

Nancy changed the subject. "I'm curious, Evelyn. Why do you have five Christmas trees?"

"Actually there are six. Thank goodness, one is still on stage. *Alias Angel Divine,* Joseph's brilliant play, takes place over six different Christmases, each two years apart—"

"It's a *wonderful* play," Marla gushed. Both she and Evelyn seemed determined to boost Joseph's morale. "It's about a chorus girl who *claws* her way to the top." She raked her long red-painted nails in the air, sending cigarette ashes flying. *"Quite authentic.* Believe me, I've met more than one of those wildcats in my time."

"My character Angel is not just 'one of those wildcats,' Marla," Joseph said. "She's unique. That would be clear if Evelyn would direct the play the way I intended—"

"Please, Joseph, this really isn't the time to argue about my direction!" Evelyn shivered. "Come on, let's head for the Lodge." She asked the security guards to stay until they were sure the last embers were out. "I'm hungry. What about you?"

Nancy had been poking through the ruins with a long stick. She stooped to gather up a few half-burned papers. "What are these?" she asked.

Joseph studied the scraps. "Old scripts," he pronounced. "Earlier versions of *Angel.*"

"Why would they be in the shed?"

He shrugged. "Who knows? Probably got mixed in with a box of props. They're of no use now."

Unless some of them had been used to start the fire, Nancy thought.

She followed the others down the hill and up the steps into the main room of the Lodge. They were greeted by the smell of something good cooking and the sound of carols playing in the background. The right-hand part of the long room was a dining area with enough tables to seat several dozen people. The left was a lounge containing a pool table, big-screen TV, and comfortable chairs near a stone fireplace, now ablaze with a cheery fire. Ruby candles glowed on the mantel, ropes of evergreen boughs tied with gold bows hung from the rustic wooden beams, and a huge Christmas tree surrounded by presents stood at the far end of the room.

"That's a really dumb idea, Sherri," Fiona Sweeney was saying to the stocky girl who had decorated the prop trees. They were standing near the front door.

"But it would be so much easier," Sherri replied in a reasonable tone.

"I'm not taking the Christmas decorations from here to use on stage." Fiona put her hands on her hips. "Just because you don't want to do the extra work—"

"I didn't say that. We don't mind, do we?" Sherri looked at the rest of the crew, who were watching the argument. They all chimed in, agreeing with her.

"Fine, then keep your brilliant ideas to yourself." Fiona turned her back on the group and stalked over to the pool table. She racked the balls, then picked up a cue and began to sink them with expert precision.

Evelyn took Nancy aside. "I don't know why Fiona has been on edge lately. Usually the crew and apprentices adore her. I've considered telling her about the threats, but she's been so tense . . ."

"Do you think she might have something to do with the notes?"

"Fiona? Absolutely not! Never! She's been with me since the beginning. She came here to work as an apprentice right out of high school."

"Have you seen my knitting, Evelyn?" Marla asked, appearing behind Nancy. "I left it here, I'm sure."

"Maybe it's at the house." Evelyn smiled at Marla, but Nancy could tell she was upset.

"Soup's on!" a woman in a long white apron

sang out as she pushed through the kitchen doors carrying a heavy tray. Everyone flocked to the dining area. Nancy and her friends joined Evelyn and Marla at a round table set apart from the ones where everyone else had gathered.

Dinner was served family style. Ned had just passed Nancy a bowl of rich dark stew when the front door opened and two people—one tiny, one tall—blew in with a gust of damp air. The woman threw back the hood of her burgundy cloak and masses of dark curls tumbled around her shoulders. As the tall man helped her remove the cloak, the raven hair spilled over a pink silk blouse, down to the waistband of her perfectly cut slacks.

"Size two, or I'll eat my fork," George muttered in Nancy's ear.

Nancy nodded, staring at the young woman. Her perfect face featured a rosebud mouth, almond-shaped olive eyes, and the flawless skin usually seen only in baby lotion commercials. Could she be for real? Nancy caught herself wondering.

One glance at Ned told Nancy he was thinking the same thing. Nancy changed her focus to the tall man. He, too, was gorgeous, a brown-eyed blond with a strong jaw. He unzipped his windbreaker, revealing a lean figure. It was Brent of "Ventura Boulevard."

"Matt, Laura, you're just in time for Emily's famous stew," Evelyn called.

"Evelyn, darling, the prop shed!" The dark-haired beauty floated over to the table. "We saw it. How are we going to rehearse tomorrow?"

"The crew will start working on replacement props tonight," Evelyn said. "Let's not spoil Emily's delicious dinner by worrying about it now. I want you to meet George Fayne and her friends."

As Evelyn made the introductions, Nancy marveled over the woman's ability to be gracious and collected in the face of trouble. She really was an incredible actress, Nancy thought.

Matt Duncan took the chair next to George. George, normally cool and composed, turned pink when Matt accidentally brushed her arm.

"I don't know if I can handle it, Evelyn," Matt said as he unfolded his napkin. "You know I've built my performance around specific props. I pick up the plain white plate in scene one and say, 'You look worried tonight, Angel.' I pick up the holly plate in scene two and say, 'You look lovely tonight, darling.' Without them, I'm not sure I'll be able to remember which scene I'm in."

"You'll be fine, Matt." Evelyn passed him the basket of biscuits. "I guarantee your stage fright will vanish once the curtain rises."

"But this is a *live* audience. No cuts, no re-takes. What happens if I go up on my lines?" he said.

"I'll help you out, darling," Laura cooed. "Did

I ever tell you about the time I was in *The Miracle Worker* and Roy Morrison suddenly jumped twenty pages ahead in the script?"

As Laura told one story after another, Nancy discovered that the young actress had been in show business since she was a child. Laura scattered around the names of the rich and famous like sprinkles on a sugar cookie. Ned watched her, fascinated, and Nancy watched him watching her.

Nancy was also aware of George's problem. Sitting next to Brent was apparently more painful than pleasurable for her. She mumbled brief answers when he politely asked her a few questions, then ate her dinner in stiff silence.

Not that Matt was talkative. He seemed preoccupied and stammered a little whenever Evelyn tried to include him in the conversation. Nancy wondered if he was worried about the play or if something else was bothering him.

When dessert was served, Laura began asking Marla's opinion on a scene. "Evelyn agrees that my character would never admit to Michael that she played a dirty trick. I have the script right here. What do you think?"

Marla searched her pockets. "Now *where* did I leave my glasses? I know, I must have left them in the theater."

"Never mind, you can read it in the morning."

"No, no, no. I'd better get them now. Maybe that's where I left my knitting, too." Marla stubbed out her cigarette and turned to Nancy. "You haven't seen the Barn yet. Would you like a little tour?"

"I'd love it." Nancy glanced at Ned. "Why don't you come, too?" She squeezed his hand.

"Uh, sure," Ned said. "Back in a little while." He smiled at Laura.

"I'll come, too!" George stood up so quickly she almost knocked her chair over. "I'm dying to see the Barn."

As they left the Lodge, Nancy breathed deeply. The rain had stopped and the night air smelled damp and woodsy. Marla led them to the main door of the theater, used her key to open the lock, and began snapping on lights.

"The lobby is small but welcoming, don't you think? Evelyn did a marvelous job redecorating." She opened double doors and turned on more lights. Rows of seats stretched down to the stage, where a living room set was half in shadow. A tall metal ladderlike scaffold had been pushed to one side of the set. Nancy assumed the crew climbed up it to adjust the lights high above the stage.

Marla trotted down the aisle. "I'll turn on the work lights, so you can see the set. It's *simply magnificent.* Follow me."

George lingered behind as Nancy and Ned trailed after Marla and went up a side ramp leading to the stage. "Careful of the rug." Marla paused and pointed, then continued. "They should tape it down—"

Despite her own warning, Marla then stumbled on the rug. Nancy was on the ramp when she saw her pitch forward.

Then Nancy heard a loud crash and then a creaking sound.

Marla shrieked.

Nancy raised her eyes in time to see the heavy scaffold begin to tip toward the stage and Marla.

Chapter Three

NANCY AND NED shot forward and grabbed Marla's ankles as the scaffold continued collapsing toward the floor. Desperately, the two tugged her to the front of the stage.

The iron bars crashed to the floor just as they were clear, missing Marla by inches.

Nancy knelt beside her. "Are you all right?"

Marla opened her eyes. Her face was white. "I think so," she whispered. "What happened?"

"You tripped. Did you hit your head when you fell?" Nancy asked.

Marla touched her forehead. "I don't know. Maybe . . . no, I don't think so."

"Lie still for a few minutes. You've had a nasty shock." Nancy made her as comfortable as possible with a cushion from the couch on the set.

Satisfied that Marla only needed time to recover, Nancy asked George to stay with the older woman while she and Ned surveyed the damage. The scaffold had missed the only surviving Christmas tree, but the rest of the set was a wreck. Tables and chairs were crushed, and vases, mirrors, and pictures lay scattered and broken.

"What a mess," Ned said, shaking his head.

Nancy found a switch on a panel just offstage, turned on overhead strips of fluorescent lights, and inspected the scaffold. She noticed a gleam on one of the top bars. "What's this?" she asked as she felt a thin plastic wire. "Fishing line!"

She grabbed a flashlight from a table backstage and began to trace the strong transparent wire. She followed it up to a rafter, where it passed through a pulley, then across to another rafter and pulley, and then back down to the floor.

"Ned, it's a booby trap," Nancy said. "Marla must have tripped on the wire where it was stretched across the stage and tied to that weight." She pointed offstage to a cinder block at the end of the line. The block lay on the floor, but Nancy guessed that it had been perched on the low bench that sat beside it before Marla tripped on the wire and sent the block toppling. "That was the crash we heard," she told Ned.

She went over to the cinder block and shone her flashlight directly above it. "The line that starts at the scaffold and goes over the rafters must have been tied to the block, and the dropping block yanked the wire—"

"Forcing the scaffold to tip," Ned said, finishing her thought.

"Someone's too smart for their own good," Nancy said.

The actress was sitting up now, although she was still pale. "Why would anyone want to hurt *me?"* she asked.

"We don't know that the trap was set for you," Nancy answered. "Who would guess that you'd come back to the theater tonight? It may have been set for someone else—or no one in particular." She looked at the smashed set. "Maybe it was just another attempt to stop the play."

"I wonder if the person who wrote the notes and set the fires is behind this," George said.

Nancy turned to her friend. "I don't know. But we've got to tell Evelyn."

Marla stood up. "Poor darling—as if she doesn't have enough problems."

"Don't forget your glasses," George said. "I found them on an aisle seat."

"My glasses?" Marla said vaguely. "Oh, yes. Thank you, dear."

When they arrived back at the Lodge, they saw that the crew was getting ready to get to work. Nancy and Marla took Evelyn aside and told her what had happened.

"Oh, no!" Evelyn put her arm around Marla. "Are you sure you're all right?"

"Yes, only a little shaken. I'll be fine."

"Evelyn," Nancy said. "We have to report this to the police. Marla was almost killed."

Evelyn acted stricken. "But they'll close us down if they find out." She clasped her hands together tightly. "Oh, Nancy, I know you can get to the bottom of this. I'm counting on you."

"I'll certainly try, but the police—"

"No police. Please, Nancy."

Nancy frowned, then sighed.

Evelyn suddenly became brisk and determined. "We'll hold our own investigation. Since we can't let on that you're a detective, I'll ask the questions. Tell me exactly what you need to know."

Nancy told her and Evelyn nodded. "Attention, everyone." She strode to the fireplace. "I'm afraid I have some bad news. Come sit down. I need to talk to you."

Mumbling things like "More bad news?" and "What else could go wrong?" the cast and crew sat down.

Evelyn tried to smile at the apprehensive crew. "The good news is, the sixth Christmas tree has not been damaged. The bad news is, the set has suffered—a bit." She went on to explain what had happened. Once the shocked reaction had died down, she continued. "The trap was obviously set between the end of rehearsal and dinner. I'll need to know who was the last out of the theater and where each of you went after leaving it. Also, does anyone recall sticking outdated scripts in the prop shed?"

One by one Evelyn went around to speak to the company. Nancy took this opportunity to sort out who was who on the crew and what their activities had been before the fire in the prop shed. Fiona had been the last to leave, with Sherri, the stocky girl who was stage-managing the play. They had turned off the lights in the theater and joined the set designer, Jill, in the production office off the lobby to figure out how to manage a few fast set and prop changes. The company's two young apprentices were also there. Jerry, the lanky guy who was in charge of lights, had gone to the Lodge to play pool with Ben, chief of set construction, and Howie, the box office manager.

Laura had been in her cabin, conferring with Liz, the costume designer. Marla had also been in the Lodge. She'd watched the pool game for a while, then decided to read by the fire. Realizing she'd left her glasses at the Barn, she went out into the rain to get them. This was when she had seen the shed on fire. After alerting the crew and guards, she ran to tell Evelyn.

Only Joseph Brunner, who claimed to be in his cabin working on rewrites, and Matt Duncan, who'd driven Evelyn's car to the pharmacy in town, were without alibis.

No one remembered putting old scripts in the shed, but everyone agreed it was possible they'd been shoved in a box of props.

As soon as the questioning was over, Fiona hurried her crew to the Barn to see what could be salvaged. After checking out the damage, Matt, Joseph, and Laura decided a game of bridge would help them relax.

"Ned," Laura asked sweetly, "are you good at bridge? I'm really pretty bad at it, but if you'll be my partner, I know we could win."

"Okay," Ned said affably, missing the look that Nancy threw him.

"Would you like to unpack?" Evelyn asked George and Nancy. "I'll show you to your cabins."

"I'd rather check out the computer in the office first, if you don't mind." Nancy's tone implied that *some* people had important work to do. Ned didn't seem to hear her.

"All right." Evelyn took Nancy and George back up to the Barn and into the small production office off the lobby. She showed Nancy the computer, then went into the theater to confer with Fiona while Nancy experimented with the printer.

"Everything is identical to the anonymous notes," Nancy told George. "Of course, this printer is a popular brand, so the notes could have been run off anywhere else."

"It *must* be someone from outside," George said. "No one in the company would have a motive for destroying the play or the Red Barn."

"What about the neighbor that Evelyn mentioned—Charles Ferguson?" Nancy asked. "He wants to buy this place, and she said she'd have to sell if the play was canceled. I want to talk to him."

They found Evelyn onstage, assessing the damage with Fiona, who was in a surprisingly good mood.

After the women finished, Evelyn grabbed some flashlights and helped Nancy and George unload their stuff. She took them down a narrow wooded path along the river to the cabins where they'd be staying. All the crew and cast members were housed in these cabins.

"I was surprised that Fiona wasn't angry any longer," Nancy told Evelyn. "You'd think the condition of the set would have upset her."

Evelyn chuckled. "That's our Fiona. She's a real pro and loves a challenge."

"You don't think . . ." Nancy paused to phrase her question carefully. "That she was pleased to see the set destroyed? That maybe she doesn't want this play to open?"

"Of course not! Fiona would *never* do such a thing. I know she was unhappy when I chose this play, but once she takes on a job, she commits herself to it completely."

"Why doesn't she like the play?" Nancy was surprised by this new bit of information.

"I'm not positive—she didn't explain. But she did try to convince me not to do it—even threatened to quit. I managed to talk her out of it."

"Does Joseph Brunner have a lot of enemies? Maybe someone wants to keep him from having a hit with his new play?" Nancy suggested.

Evelyn shrugged. "I think he's just nervous and a bit paranoid—not unlike many play-wrights before an opening," she added, grinning.

They reached a clearing with twelve small cabins scattered around it in no apparent pat-tern. Evelyn directed the beam of her flashlight at one of the doors. "I've put you in Number Seven, George, and Nancy, you're right next door in Number Eight. Ned's across the way in Cabin Twelve. We can get him settled in later." She unlocked the door and turned on the lights.

"Wow, this is nice," George said. "Pine floors, checked curtains, rag rug—it's so New En-gland."

Evelyn laughed. "You *are* in New England, my dear. Years ago this place was a summer camp. Can you believe they crammed four bunk beds and eight kids into each of these little cabins? I have the old pictures."

"Wow!" George looked around. "I'd say it was just the right size for one person now. Perfect, in fact."

"Well, I do put the two apprentices together. I'd better get back to the theater."

"Evelyn, before you go," Nancy said, "I need to ask you about Charles Ferguson. What sort of person is he?"

"Rich!" Evelyn said.

"What else can you tell me?"

"I have never met him. He moved in last spring, and so far I've only dealt with his lawyers. I gather he made a fortune in real estate and thinks that money can buy anything."

"Why does he want your land?" Nancy asked.

"He hasn't said, but he seems absolutely determined to buy it."

"Is there a possibility he could be behind the threats and fires?"

Evelyn frowned. "I don't know. I suspect he's rather ruthless in business, but—"

"I'd like to meet him tomorrow," Nancy said.

"All right, I'll call to make an appointment." She seemed thoughtful. "I have to get back. Sleep well."

After Evelyn left, Nancy asked George to join her in her cabin as soon as she unpacked. A short while later both girls were curled up on Nancy's bed, sipping the hot chocolate Nancy had made on the cabin's hot plate.

"One suspect is Charles Ferguson," Nancy said, beginning a list in her notebook. "We need to find out more about him, ASAP."

"Agreed," George said. "Another is Fiona Sweeney, who must know all about special effects, including how to rig that scaffold."

"But she has an alibi for the time from the end of rehearsal to the beginning of dinner. Two people say she was with them."

"Maybe they're covering for her," George suggested.

"Why? Unless they're involved, too. I'll have to question them again. Right now we should focus on the two people who were alone. They can't prove where they were. Brunner could have slipped out of his cabin. No one would have known."

"Yeah, the cabins are isolated." George looked at the dark window, but saw only the room reflected back at her.

"And Matt—not only doesn't he have an alibi, he's also behaving suspiciously."

"What do you mean?" George sat up straight.

"He seemed so nervous at dinner. He says it's stage fright, but it could—"

"No way!" George said. "Of course it's stage fright! He's probably never been in front of a live audience before. I'd be terrified, too."

"George, I know you have a crush on him, but—"

"Me? A crush?" George snapped. "I have no crush on him. I just happen to think he's a wonderful actor."

"Who's also ultrahandsome," Nancy teased.

"That's not funny!" George jumped up.

"Take it easy. I only meant—"

"I know what you meant, and it's not true!" George grabbed her coat, jerked open the door, and ran to her own cabin.

For a minute Nancy stood at the threshold. George rarely flew off the handle. Obviously, she'd fallen for Matt and didn't know how to handle it.

Nancy wished she could take back her words. She closed the door and leaned against it. Poor George, she thought. First thing in the morning she'd talk to her. In the meantime it was best to let her cool down and relax.

Nancy glanced at her watch. It was late. Where was Ned? Still playing cards in the Lodge? She wanted to discuss what had just happened with him. He'd understand.

She was headed for the bathroom to brush her teeth when she heard singing outside.

"Jingle bells, jingle bells, jingle all the way. Oh, what fun—" Pressing her face up close to the window she could make out Ned and Laura strolling down the path singing. Ned had his carry-on bag slung over his shoulder.

"Great," Nancy muttered. "Just great." She slammed the bathroom door behind her and took out her frustration on her teeth, brushing furiously.

When she went back into the main room, feeling slightly calmer, she found an envelope lying on her bed.

She picked it up, opened it, and froze.

The note read: I know who you are. Stop playing with fire. Go home before you get burned.

Chapter Four

NANCY FLUNG OPEN the door. The clearing was empty, although lights shone out from several cabin windows. She grabbed a flashlight to check for footprints, but the muddy ground had been tracked by too many feet.

Back in the cabin, she studied the note, another computer printout, identical to the others.

"Go home?" she said out loud. "Not until I find out who you are. And I will, believe me." In spite of her resolve, however, she lay awake in the dark, thinking about the first sentence: "I know who you are." Only Evelyn, Marla, and the guards knew that. Had someone else recognized her? Who? And how?

The next morning Nancy caught her breath as she peered out the window. A sudden freeze had swept over the rain-soaked world and turned it into a fairyland. Sparkling ice coated every branch, twig, and blade of grass. The bright sun turned each tiny ice drop into a rainbow prism.

After dressing quickly, Nancy hurried to Ned's cabin. She knocked and after a moment he opened the door a crack. His hair mussed, his eyes barely open, he told her he'd meet her at the Lodge. Annoyed, Nancy said she'd be waiting.

When George opened her door, Nancy's arm swept over the landscape. "Isn't it beautiful?"

George blinked, trying to adjust her eyes to the brilliant light. "I had the shades down. Wow, what happened?"

"Magic! Hurry and finish dressing. I'm starved."

George glanced down at her feet. "Um, you go ahead."

"You're not still mad at me, are you?" Nancy asked. "I'm really sorry. Will you forgive me?"

"Oh, sure," George said vaguely before turning away. "Come on in while I get ready."

Nancy sat on the bed. "You don't sound very happy. I wish I could take back everything I said last night."

"It's not your fault," George mumbled as she pulled a heavy blue sweater over her head. "It's just that Matt makes me feel like such an idiot. I get all knotted up inside and can't think of a single thing to say to him. It's so—stupid!"

"I understand, but you have to remind yourself

that he's just a guy who happens to make his living as an actor."

"Right. So why am I making a fool of myself over him?" George reached into the closet for her leather boots.

"You're not! I don't think anyone noticed except me, and that's only because I know you so well. Look, just relax and treat him like an ordinary person—"

"Who just happens to be ultrahandsome." George jammed her foot into a boot. "And famous all over the country—"

"And who still puts *his* boots on one foot at a time, just like you do."

George laughed lightly. "You're right. I'll try."

Nancy grinned. "You'll be fine. Trust me."

While they walked to the Lodge through the woods beside the river, Nancy told George about the note she had found on her bed.

"I can't believe it. That means someone walked right into your cabin while you were brushing your teeth," George said.

"I think I would have noticed the note if it had been there when I first came in," Nancy agreed.

"Maybe someone recognized you from a previous case," George suggested.

"I'm positive I've never met anyone here before. I wonder if someone could have overheard us talking?"

"Well, I'll keep my ears open to hear if anyone drops a hint about your being a detective."

"Good." Nancy nodded. "I was going to ask you to watch rehearsal this morning, anyway. Keep your eye on Joseph Brunner and Fiona. According to Evelyn, she's been unusually tense and angry lately. See if you can find out why her behavior is so volatile."

"Sure. But I hope she's not involved. I kind of like her."

No one was talking at the Lodge. It was almost too quiet. Fiona and the crew were probably too tired to speak since they'd been up most of the night. Joseph was making notes in his script. Only Evelyn and Marla were talking—and they whispered.

Breakfast was relaxed until Matt arrived to take his seat. He sat down next to George again. "Good morning," he said, smiling at her.

George flashed Nancy a look of panic, then said quietly, "Morning." She suddenly became very busy with her waffle, pouring syrup into each and every hole.

Fortunately, Matt was too preoccupied with his script to notice.

Ned arrived and had just sat down when a loud crash sounded.

Nancy saw two plates upside down on the table in front of Matt and George. Yellow flecks of scrambled egg dotted the tablecloth.

Everyone stared at Matt and George, who seemed to be frozen in place.

Suddenly they both lifted their heads and their

eyes met. Then they burst out laughing. Matt was laughing so hard Nancy thought she could detect tears in his eyes.

Finally Matt began to explain, "She was passing me the—" He broke off, chuckling again.

"Just as he passed me—" George gasped out.

"And my plate hit her plate—" Matt mimed the two plates colliding.

"And *wham!*" George giggled. "Are you going to send us to our rooms, Aunt Evelyn?"

Evelyn grinned. "I should, you naughty children. How many times have I told you not to play with your food?"

That set George and Matt off again and, one by one, the others joined in. Only Joseph sat silently, frowning.

George and Matt chatted easily during the rest of breakfast. From the snatches of their conversation that Nancy overheard, she could tell that George was doing her best to reassure the insecure actor that he'd be great in the show.

As soon as Ned finished eating, Nancy took him outside and explained what she planned to do. While George was in the theater, they would check out the compound for any clues.

They caught the groundskeeper, Ed, as he was coming out of the Lodge. They asked if he could show them around, and he was more than happy to oblige.

They stood on the Lodge's riverside porch, looking out at the river. "She's running fast now," Ed said, "with all the rain we've had."

To their right was Evelyn's house, also overlooking the cold blue water. Beyond it, Nancy saw a stable with two beautiful horses, a chestnut and a bay, in the paddock.

To their left was the path to the cabins. The narrow trail was bounded by woods on one side and a steep drop to the river on the other. "That trail keeps going," Ed said, "all the way into Bridgeville and eventually to Long Island Sound."

He took them along another path that led to the theater. The burned prop shed was an ugly black scar in the ice-covered ground. There was a parking lot on the far side of the Barn and large sheds between the theater and the woods. One housed the workshop where sets were built; another held racks of costumes and a small sewing area.

"Why were so many of the props being used in this show kept in the shed that burned?" Nancy asked Ed. "Why not in the theater?"

"I'll show you." Ed led them to the rear door of the Barn, into the backstage area. "See, back here you've got your dressing rooms and your greenroom with a coffee maker, fridge, and chairs." They walked down a short corridor that gave way to the stage. "Then you've got your offstage area." He pointed out a narrow, crowded space on the side of the set already filled with props and furniture.

The stage manager, Sherri, was sitting there on a stool near heavy black curtains. She was wearing a headset and held a board with various gadgets attached to wires. As they watched, she pressed a button and a doorbell rang. Matt and Laura's voices carried through the curtains from the stage.

"I see," Nancy whispered. "There sure isn't room for six Christmas trees, is there? I had no idea the backstage area was so small. The Barn seems so big from the outside."

"If you had planned it," Ed asked as they returned to the corridor outside the greenroom, "what would you do? Put in as many seats as you could for the audience or give your crew a nice big prop room?"

"You seem to know a lot about theater," Nancy said, smiling.

"Well, now, I've been known to do my bit. Not as much as the likes of them, of course," he said, pointing in the direction of the stage.

"Thanks for the tour, Ed," Nancy said. "Now I want to take a closer look at the burned shed," she said to Ned.

Nancy and Ned went back outside and poked around the ruins. Gradually Nancy expanded the search. About twenty feet away in a cluster of pine trees she found an empty kerosene can lying under a bush. She picked it up. It was rusted and caked with wet leaves.

"It looks like it's been here for months," Ned said.

"Yes," Nancy agreed. "And even if it was used to start the fire in the shed and tossed here yesterday, we'd never be able to find fingerprints on it." Then she stopped and thought. "But I'm going to hang on to it, anyway, just in case."

She and Ned stashed the can in Nancy's cabin.

The sun was melting the ice and the trees were dripping by the time they returned to the theater to see how rehearsal was going.

"Oh, boy," George said when they sat down next to her near the back of the theater. "They call this a 'tech,' but I call it a mess. Everything's going wrong."

"What does 'tech' mean?" Ned asked.

"It's short for technical rehearsal. The crew is trying to get the lighting and sound cues coordinated."

"Hold it!" Evelyn called from the front row. "Jerry, downstage right is still in shadow. Can you fix it?"

"I'll try," the lighting man called from the booth on their right. One side of the stage suddenly lit up brightly.

"I said downstage *right,* not left." Evelyn's voice was patient. The too-bright area dimmed, but nothing else happened. "What's the problem?"

"We're going to have to refocus," Jerry said. "Ben, get the scaffold."

The actors continued, working around Ben, who scrambled up and down the scaffold with a big wrench, adjusting the angle of the lights.

"Laura plays Angel Divine," George whispered. "This is the third scene, and she's just auditioned for a Hollywood producer. Matt is her boyfriend, and he doesn't want her to move to California."

There was a sudden pause in the dialogue. Matt rolled his eyes. "I *said,* I can't just pick up and move west. *My job is here.*"

Silence.

"Where is the telephone?" Matt shouted. "The stupid phone is supposed to ring as soon as I say, 'My job is here!' "

Silence.

"What's the problem, Sherri?" Evelyn said.

"There's something wrong with the connection." She poked her head out around the curtain.

"That's it! I've had it!" Matt threw his script down. "Not once has that phone rung on cue. Call me when you have finally made the connection!" He stalked off the stage, past the anxious stage manager.

No one said a word for a moment, then Evelyn said calmly, "He'll be fine once he cools down. Fiona, would you read Matt's lines?"

Fiona, who was sitting next to her, stood up and began to take off her headset.

"Fiona, darling," Laura said softly from the stage. "I'd really rather have a man read. It's much easier for Angel to relate to a man."

"Jerry's running the light board," Fiona said. "Ben is busy, as you can see, and Howie's in the box office. I'm afraid you'll have to make do with me."

"Well, what about Ned?" Laura smiled gently. "Would you be willing to help out, Ned, darling?"

"But I'm not an actor," he said.

"Oh, please," Laura begged. "I'm sure you'll be very good at it."

He stood up slowly. "Well, I did do a commercial once. Would you like me to fill in, Evelyn?"

"Why not give it a try?" she answered. "I really need Fiona backstage, anyway."

Ned loped down the aisle, ran up on stage, and picked up Matt's script. Laura helped him find the place. She was standing a little closer than was really necessary, Nancy thought.

"Why don't we pick it up after the phone call?" she suggested sweetly.

Nancy watched Ned read the scene, amazed that Laura had talked him into it. He'd never shown any interest in acting before, but she had to admit he did look awfully handsome up there.

Sometime later Nancy realized that George

was gone. Shrugging, she focused on the play. Ned was beginning to read pretty well as he came to understand the character and what the scene required. Eventually, the phone did ring on cue.

Just as the crew began to cheer, the theater doors banged open and George ran in, breathless and sopping wet from the thighs down. "Help! Help, everyone! Come quick! It's Matt!"

"What happened?" Evelyn jumped up.

"He fell in the river!"

Chapter Five

"I CLIMBED DOWN and pulled him out of the water." George panted. "But he's hurt and I was afraid to try to get him up the bank. Hurry!" She turned and ran out of the theater.

"Fiona, get a rope!" Evelyn ran up the aisle. "Ben, find blankets. I'll call an ambulance!"

Not waiting for the others, Nancy dashed for the river. When she reached the shaded path, she slid on a patch of ice and had to make a grab for the railing. The ice had melted in the sun, but it was still solid under the trees. Nancy made her way down the path until she finally reached a spot where the wooden guard rail was broken in two.

"Down here!" George called. She was kneeling beside Matt, who was lying on the steep rocky slope by the river.

Nancy scrambled down to him. Matt's eyes were open, and they registered his pain. "Where are you hurt?" she asked.

"My ankle," he gasped. "I think I sprained it." He was soaked to the waist, and blood trickled from a cut on his cheek.

"Does anything else hurt?"

"Not really."

Nancy took off her jacket and covered him, then gently loosened his shoelaces and pushed down his sock. The ankle was already red and swollen. "Just lie still," she told him. "Help is on the way. How did it happen?"

"I was angry, walking fast, not paying attention. Suddenly I slipped, and before I knew it I was halfway in the river." His lips were blue, and he was shivering. "Thank goodness for George."

"I went looking for him," George explained, "thinking he might want someone to talk to. Then I saw the broken railing."

Nancy raised her eyes up to the splintered rail. "You must have hit it with a lot of force, Matt."

"No. I just fell against it and it gave way."

"I'm sorry, but I have to ask you this question. Is there any chance you were pushed?"

"No! Of course not! I was all alone."

Just then some others arrived. "An ambulance will be here any minute," Evelyn called down.

"Toss us the blankets," Nancy said. "We don't want to move him in case there are broken bones. So far, it seems to be only his ankle."

Matt was still shivering when the ambulance arrived. The paramedics climbed down the embankment, checked him over, and found no injuries other than the ankle and bruises. They eased him onto the stretcher, and Nancy and George pitched in to help carry it up the slippery slope.

"I'll be back in a couple of hours," Matt told Evelyn as they lifted him into the ambulance. "Don't replace me. It's only my ankle. Promise?"

"I'm sure you'll be fine," Evelyn answered. "And we wouldn't think of replacing you."

"I'll be back in time for this afternoon's rehearsal!" were Matt's last words before the doors were closed and the ambulance drove away, siren wailing.

"Maybe I should have gone with him," George said.

"He's in good hands," Nancy assured her. "Besides, I need you here to help me figure out how he fell."

As soon as everyone left the scene, Nancy, Ned, and George inspected the railing. The wood was rotten in the section that had broken. Nancy found no sign that it had been tampered with.

"Everyone was in the theater when this happened, except for Joseph and Marla," Nancy said.

"I saw Marla in the office, working on the computer, when I went out after Matt," George said. "But I don't know where Joseph was."

"Did you question him or Fiona this morning?"

George shook her head. "Fiona was too busy, and he wasn't around. I heard someone say he was rewriting in his cabin, but I didn't want to leave the theater. What if something happened?"

"You were right," Nancy agreed. "I feel uneasy without one of us there, in case the arsonist tries again. And that means we'd better get back right now."

Ned checked his watch. "I think they're going to break for lunch just about now."

"Okay," Nancy replied. "Let's get a bite to eat ourselves."

Matt's doctor called from the hospital after lunch. His patient was fine and demanding to be released, but the ankle was badly sprained and one bone had a thin stress fracture. Matt could use crutches occasionally, but he'd have to be in a wheelchair for performances.

The company went into a huddle in the Lodge. It was too late to replace Matt, even if he'd allow it. A small theater like the Red Barn couldn't afford to hire understudies. Also, the audience was coming to see Matt Duncan, not a replacement. They came to the only logical conclusion—the play would have to be blocked to accommodate his wheelchair.

"Think of it this way," Marla said. "It's a simply *marvelous* opportunity for publicity. I can see the headlines: 'Star injured, the play goes on.'

I'm going to call the newspapers and TV stations. We'll set up a press conference for late this afternoon."

"Do we need more publicity? The box office is almost sold out," Evelyn said.

"'*Almost*'? We'll have them banging down the doors." Marla rubbed her hands. "When I did *Plaza Suite* in Phoenix with what's-his-name . . . the dark guy with the mustache . . . you know who I mean. He showed up with his arm in a cast one day. Sales were sluggish so he pulled the old show-must-go-on bit and, *boom,* they went through the *roof.* Just one problem—he wasn't hurt at all! *Faked* the whole thing!" She laughed.

Evelyn barely smiled. "Well, we have our work cut out for us. Ned, would you mind filling in for Matt again? We'll put you in a chair, move you around, so we can start refocusing lights at least."

He nodded and she continued. "I'll call Matt and tell him. Now, anyone not needed in the theater has plenty to do on the props. Jill and Ben, go into town to buy whatever we need. Take my car. The keys are under the front seat."

People hurried off in different directions. Evelyn started for the Barn, and Nancy and George caught up to her. "Can we help?" Nancy offered.

Evelyn considered, then said, "Thanks, but we can handle it." She paused. "On second thought, there is one favor I'd like to ask. My horses haven't been exercised for several days, thanks to all the confusion. I know George is an excellent rider, and she told me you are, too."

"Well, yes," Nancy said. "But I'm not sure I should leave the compound—"

"Just for an hour. The radio says snow is on the way, and the poor dears are so restless. George, you take Bravo and, Nancy, you'll like Applause. Give them a good long canter, and I'll be forever grateful."

She led them to the stable. It was hard to resist the two beautiful horses waiting in the paddock. Bravo was a big chestnut gelding, and the mare, Applause, a pretty bay. Evelyn left, and while George and Nancy saddled up, the horses pawed at the ground, eager to be off.

"I don't know," Nancy said, tightening the girth. "I feel uneasy about leaving the compound."

George glanced up at the sky. Thick clouds had rolled in, and the temperature was dropping. "Sure looks like snow. Before it hits, this guy needs to have a little fun, don't you, fellow?" She stroked his coppery neck. "Don't worry, Nan, we'll be back in an hour."

"Well, all right." Nancy mounted. They walked down the driveway, the horses dancing in anticipation. After they crossed the road they found a break in the stone wall bordering a large field and let the horses out into a canter.

Nancy's mare fell into place behind the gelding. She had a smooth rolling stride that Nancy adjusted to easily. George had more difficulty keeping Bravo from bolting into a gallop.

"This is one wild horse!" George called, laughing. The wind whipped the words over her shoulder.

Keeping the road on their right, they cantered up a long slope and down the far side, then skirted a stand of trees until they found a wide path through the woods. Jumping a shallow creek here and a low wall there, they rode up and down the hills, as exhilarated as the horses. The sharp air reddened their cheeks, and their breath came out in frosty puffs.

Finally they paused to rest, and Nancy noticed that a few soft snowflakes were swirling from the sky. "We'd better head back," she told George.

"Gosh, I hate to," George said. "This big guy could run all day, but I guess you're right."

They trotted back to the road, then slowed to a walk. Bravo kept trying to break into a faster gait, but George's hands were firm on the reins.

"I'm worried about this case," Nancy said. "First, I'm not convinced that Matt wasn't pushed."

"But why would he lie?" George asked. "To protect someone? Who?"

"I don't know."

"Come on, Nan, you've trusted my instincts before. I'm sure Matt's telling the truth."

"Okay, I'll agree with you, but he can only tell the truth as he knows it. Maybe he didn't realize he was being pushed—or he's forgotten."

"That's right. Shock can do that sometimes."

Nancy brushed snow from Applause's mane. "This is the second accident. The first one was definitely planned. Marla was almost killed in that booby trap, but we don't know that she was the intended victim."

"Easy, boy." George reined in the big, frisky horse. "And we don't know that the arsonist is the same one who set the trap."

"Let's assume for the moment it's one person and focus on alibis. I checked with Sherri and Jill at lunch. They repeated that Fiona was with them and I believe them. That leaves Joseph and—"

"And Matt. Nancy, I just can't believe he would do such a thing. Besides, today *he* was the victim of an accident."

"Let's keep an open mind about him."

George frowned. "If you're going to include victims in your suspicions, what about Marla?"

"If we think in terms of two different suspects, one who rigs booby traps and one who sets fires, she's a possibility," Nancy commented.

"But she's so forgetful," George said. "If she tried to set fire to the Barn, she'd probably end up burning the Lodge down instead."

Nancy laughed.

"Besides," George added, "why would she do it?"

"Motive is the problem. Within the company, no one stands to gain by destroying the Barn, with the possible exception of Fiona. We know she was upset when Evelyn chose this play, and she didn't want to work on it. We have to find out why."

"I'll try to talk to her." George reined back her horse as he broke into a trot. "Easy, easy. The road's too slippery, Bravo."

The snow was falling thick and fast now, the ground already coated white.

"Meanwhile," Nancy said, "I want to dig into the neighbor's background. Evelyn tried to call Ferguson this morning, but he was out."

"Don't forget our playwright, Joseph Brunner. He has no alibi, and he's kind of weird."

"Weird, yes, but why would he destroy his own play? And Evelyn thinks it's unlikely that anyone would want to do something like that to him. But I'm going to talk to him as soon as we get back. If I can't get anywhere with him, I think we should call in the police. First Marla was almost killed, now Matt's been hurt. We can't take any more chances."

"You're right." George squinted, trying to see through the swirling snow. "The road curves up ahead. We must be getting close to the turnoff to the Barn—"

A dark car suddenly appeared out of the whiteness, rushing toward them like a locomotive. Instead of slowing, it picked up speed.

Nancy dug her heels in the bay's sides, urging her to run. The mare dashed to the side of the road, then reared as she faced a high fence. Nancy pulled down on the reins, bringing the horse's head low while she struggled to stay in the saddle.

The car rushed by, almost striking George and Bravo. Neighing in fear, the chestnut whirled and bolted. In two strides he jumped and cleared the top of the wall.

George, thrown off balance, lost her stirrups. Bravo broke into a full gallop, his outstretched neck yanking the reins free.

Nancy managed to settle her horse, then swung her in a wide circle and pointed her toward the fence. "Go for it, Applause, go!"

Horse and rider sailed over the wall, landing without a stumble. Nancy spotted Bravo racing through the snow, headed for a stand of trees. If he galloped through the woods, George could be swept off his back. George had no way to control Bravo—she had no reins or stirrups. All she could do was cling to the neck of the powerful horse as he thundered into the distance.

Chapter Six

NANCY URGED THE MARE into a gallop and they pounded after the gelding. Snow whipped her face, making her eyes water, but she did see George find the stirrups with her feet just before she reached the trees. Maybe now Bravo would respond, even without reins.

A moment later Bravo veered to the right, skimming past the woods and heading for open country. Nancy turned Applause to try to cut him off. The mare gained a little on him, but couldn't catch up with the long-legged chestnut.

Blinking away tears and snowflakes, Nancy watched as George tried to grab Bravo's reins, which were caught in the mane near his head. They were just out of reach. Nancy gasped as George rose up in the stirrups. No, George, she thought, it's too dangerous. Let him run.

George almost seemed to hear her. She settled back in the saddle, crouched low. The horses galloped across fields, up and down rolling hills, jumping ditches and stone walls. Nancy prayed that neither horse would stumble.

The snow thickened and Nancy could barely keep George in sight. Finally, when Applause gradually closed the distance, she realized Bravo was beginning to slow. As she caught up, Nancy saw that George had managed to grab the reins and was now easing the horse down to a walk.

"What a ride!" George called as Nancy rode up. She was breathing heavily.

"I didn't know if you could hang on!" Nancy said.

The chestnut tossed his head and whinnied. "It was close," George said. "Did you get a good look at that car? I'm sure it tried to run us down."

"I saw part of the license plate, and I know it was a dark sedan, but I'm not sure what make the car was."

"Me neither." George shrugged. "Come on, we'd better get back to the compound."

Nancy saw only a whirling white world. Nothing was visible—not a building or road or sign. "Good idea, but where is it?"

Applause raised her head and nickered softly. "Maybe she knows," George said. "She seems to smell something."

"All right, let's see where she goes, but you'd better keep a tight rein on Bravo. He's still excited." Nancy relaxed her reins, and Applause started off at a fast walk.

They rode through the snowstorm, unable to see more than a few feet ahead. Sounds were muffled and nothing was visible. They seemed shut off from the real world.

At last they spotted a glow ahead. A light, then several lights, then a huge house emerged out of the storm. Applause broke into a trot and made straight for what turned out to be a barn. Bravo whinnied and another horse answered.

They rode into the barn and dismounted. "Let's leave them here while we go up to the house," Nancy said.

"They should be rubbed down." George brushed snow off Bravo's copper-colored coat.

"In a few minutes. We'd better ask permission before we make ourselves at home."

They walked up to the front door of the stone mansion and rang the bell. A plump lady wearing an apron opened the massive door. Nancy introduced herself and George, briefly explaining how they came to be lost. She finished by asking, "May we borrow your telephone?"

"Of course. Come with me." She led them down the hall to a book-lined study. "Mr. Ferguson, these young ladies would like to use the phone."

A wiry man in his fifties raised his head from a chair by the fireplace and peered at them over his reading glasses. "Well, hello. And who might you be?" He put down the pipe he'd been smoking and stood up. "I'm Charles Ferguson."

Nancy glanced at George, delighted to have stumbled onto one of her main suspects. She repeated her story, then called the Red Barn but didn't tell Evelyn where she was calling from or why. Evelyn assured her that everything was peaceful, or as peaceful as it could be under the circumstances. Matt had gone straight from the hospital to rehearsal. She hoped he wouldn't be too tired for the press conference she had scheduled for five o'clock.

After Nancy hung up she took a moment to study her host. Charles Ferguson was fine-boned, with a face that was all angles. Everything from his stylish haircut to the toes of his polished shoes spelled money.

His study was a blend of the old and the new, and all of it expensive. There were oriental carpets, red velvet drapes, gold-framed oil paintings, and near the bay window, a mahogany desk with a fax machine and computer.

Ferguson had been talking to George. Now he said, "Why don't you leave the horses here and let me drive you home?" He didn't wait for an answer but crossed the room and pulled a satin bell cord.

The housekeeper appeared at the door moments later. "Hilda, please tell Jenkins that the young ladies' horses are in the barn. Ask him to give them a good rubdown. We could do with a little refreshment, I think."

"Certainly, Mr. Ferguson."

"Please have a seat." He indicated a couple of heavy carved chairs. "So, you're staying at the Red Barn," he said to Nancy.

"Yes, Evelyn Caldwell is a friend of George's family. Have you met her?" she asked, knowing that he hadn't.

"No, but we've had some business contacts."

"Business?" Nancy tried to act innocent.

"I would like to acquire her property. It doesn't suit me to have a theater next door. When I bought this place last spring, I was told that the Barn was open only in the summer. Now that she's winterized it, the traffic and noise will be year-round problems. I can't have it."

Nancy was amazed at his tone. He spoke as if he was certain she would agree with him. "I didn't realize that you could hear or see the Red Barn from here. I thought we were miles away."

"You must have circled around," Ferguson said briskly. "My property line ends at the road right now. I plan to extend it all the way to the river."

"I'm not sure that Ms. Caldwell wants to sell the compound," Nancy said.

He waved his hand, as if brushing off a fly. "Anything can be bought, for the right price."

Nancy was spared having to say anything more

as the housekeeper came in with a tray of mocha coffee and dainty fruit tarts.

Ferguson switched the conversation to plans for his new estate: a swimming pool, tennis courts, a landing pad for his helicopter. "Once I add the riverfront acreage, the total value will quadruple. I'll own one of the finest properties in New England."

"That sounds—impressive," Nancy said.

"Land, Miss Drew. Put your money in land, and you'll never go wrong. I started out with one tiny lot, and look where I am now." He gazed around the room proudly.

Nancy checked her watch. "Oh, dear," she said. "I'm afraid we have to get back to the Barn for a press conference."

Ferguson helped them into their coats. "More reporters! Do you realize how many times they've called, nosing around for information about my famous neighbor?"

They walked out to the barn. One end of it had been turned into a garage for a silver sports car and a black sedan. George checked the horses, finding them comfortable in warm, roomy stalls. Nancy peeked at the sedan's license plate. She had caught only a glimpse of the partly snow-covered plate on the car that had almost run them down. But she knew that the first two numbers were rounded on the bottom and could have been 8, 3, 6, or 0. The third was straight, maybe a 1, 4, or 7.

The plate on Charles Ferguson's sedan began with 604. Nancy touched the hood. The engine was warm. Was this the car that had almost struck them?

During the slow ride back to the compound, Ferguson talked about how much he loved the Connecticut countryside. When he dropped them off in front of the theater, Nancy noted the number of cars and vans in the parking lot. In the falling snow and dim light, half the cars appeared to be dark sedans.

"What do you think?" George asked after they'd waved Charles Ferguson off. "Could he be the one threatening to burn down the barn?"

"Maybe," Nancy said. "He sure is determined to own this property, and he strikes me as the type who does what's necessary to get what he wants."

"I agree." George glanced at the lights streaming from the Lodge's windows. "Looks like the press conference has started. Let's go in."

Matt was the center of attention in his wheelchair by the fireplace. His injured foot was propped up and he was answering a reporter's question. "Yes, we in the theater say 'Break a leg' when we wish someone good luck. It hardly ever happens, though." The reporters laughed.

Marla had appointed herself MC and was enjoying the spotlight as much as Matt. With great sweeps of her hands, she called on the reporters. "Yes, darling, you in the *marvelous* little black dress."

When the interview was over and the press began to leave, Evelyn pulled Nancy into a corner. "Great news," she whispered excitedly. "I found this note in my script right after you called. Read it!"

"Ha-ha. April Fool! It was all in fun. Not to worry. Your theater is safe. Merry Christmas and have a happy New Year!"

"Isn't it wonderful?" Evelyn asked. "I feel so relieved. Angry, too, of course. Someone's been playing a very sick joke, but at least it's over, and now I can concentrate on the play."

"Evelyn," Nancy said. "I don't think you should believe this note. It may be an attempt to throw us off guard."

"But I *do* believe it. Let's be logical, Nancy. The first fire in the greenroom was obviously an accident. Anyone could have left the paper cups on the hot plate, not realizing it was turned on. It's also clear that the prop shed was hit by lightning. No sane person would try to start a fire in a thunderstorm!"

"*Sane* people do not commit arson. And rigging the booby trap with the scaffold was no accident." Nancy put her hands on her hips.

"Also, someone in a dark sedan tried to run down George, me, and your horses."

Evelyn gasped. "Were you hurt? Are the horses all right?"

"We're all fine." Nancy told her what had happened, including being driven back by Charles Ferguson. "I'm sure the car deliberately tried to hit us."

"But, Nancy, dear, isn't it just as possible the driver didn't see you? Maybe he tried to slow down but skidded in the snow."

Nancy studied Evelyn, who seemed to be determined not to face facts. Her cheeks were pink with excitement, and the frown lines on her forehead were gone. If she believed this note, she could open the play without having to worry about the audience or the Barn. She was going to ignore the evidence that Nancy knew could lead to disaster.

"Evelyn, I think we have to notify the police. These accidents—"

"No! No police. Don't you see? The danger's over, and the play opens in two days. You wait and see. Everything will be fine!"

Nancy decided not to argue with her, but was resolved to continue to investigate the case on her own until she could persuade Evelyn that the danger was real.

As Nancy left the Lodge, she saw that the snow had let up. She headed for her cabin to change her clothes. She was damp all the way through. As she passed Joseph Brunner's cabin, she heard shouting. She crept closer and peered in the window.

Fiona faced Joseph, her fist raised in fury. She screamed, "I'll kill you, you traitor! I swear I'm going to kill you."

Chapter Seven

"How could you do this to my mother? I confided in you, and you took advantage of me!" Fiona swung her fist at Brunner.

Brunner ducked, then edged behind a table that held a laptop computer and piles of papers. "Your mother is so famous that the entire country knows every detail of her life. The facts are available in any public library. I only took those facts and used my imagination—"

"You twisted the truth! You made it seem like my mother is nasty, mean, and vicious. Everyone who sees this play will think she's as awful as your Angel Divine!"

"Fiona, the whole world knows that the famous Shannon Sweeney became a superstar by stabbing a lot of people in the back—"

"My mother was ambitious!" Fiona began to

circle the table, forcing Joseph to move around it in self-defense. "But she wasn't awful—not like you've made her! And *I,* like an idiot, told you family stories when we did your last play here. Now I see those same stories acted out on stage! *You're* the one who's nasty and cruel!" She grabbed a stapler from the table and threw it at him.

Brunner jumped aside, and it crashed harmlessly into the wall. "I always write from life." He continued to circle, keeping the table between him and Fiona. "That's why I've had three hits on Broadway—"

"You and your ego!" Without warning Fiona flipped the table over. The computer crashed to the floor. Papers scattered like confetti.

"My laptop!" Joseph stared in horror.

"I'll kill you!" Fiona lunged and grabbed him by the throat.

Nancy ran to the cabin door and jerked it open. Fiona's back was to her. Nancy made a flying leap, catching her around the waist. They fell on the rug, with Nancy on top. Within seconds, Nancy had Fiona pinned to the floor.

"Let me go!" Fiona wailed. "I wasn't g-g-going to h-h-hurt him!" She began to sob.

Slowly Nancy relaxed her grip. Fiona didn't try to get up but lay on the floor, crying miserably.

"Thanks." Joseph nodded at Nancy. "I don't think she would have hurt me, but . . ." He rubbed his throat. "She's just a hothead—"

"You creep!" Fiona sobbed.

Nancy knelt by the girl and put her hand on her shoulder. "Why don't you come to my cabin? We can talk—"

"No! Leave me alone!" Fiona jumped up. "I'll get you, Brunner! I'll get even with you!" She pulled up the hood of her jacket and ran out of the cabin.

Nancy closed the door after her. "Is it true, Joseph? Did you base Angel Divine on Fiona's mother, Shannon Sweeney?"

"Yes, of course," he said brusquely. "All my characters are based on real people."

"And did you put the family stories Fiona told you in confidence into the play?"

"Of course. Why not?" He smirked.

Nancy frowned, then glanced down at the floor. "It looks like your laptop is ruined."

He picked up the computer and caressed it. "It had better not be broken. She'll pay through the nose if it is. How am I going to finish the rewrites? My program isn't compatible with that piece of junk in the office."

"Then you're familiar with the Barn's computer?"

He narrowed his eyes. "I didn't say that. Why are you asking so many questions?"

"I'm just curious. I was thinking about buying a new computer myself."

"Well, take your questions and get out. And tell that maniac to stay out of my way."

Nancy left Brunner's cabin, feeling far from sorry for him. She was sorry for Fiona, but it was clear now that she had a very strong motive for wanting to prevent the play from opening.

Nancy changed into dry clothes, then walked back toward the theater and around to the parking lot. She wanted to examine the cars that were left after the press had driven away. She found two dark sedans and jotted down their license plate numbers. One began 831, the other 067. Either one could have been the one that tried to hit them.

She wasn't able to get Evelyn alone until after dinner, a meal Nancy didn't enjoy. The lasagna was good, but Laura spoiled her appetite. Now that Ned had filled in during rehearsals, Laura seemed to think she owned him.

"Darling, you really should study acting." Laura called everyone "darling," but it sounded ominous when she was addressing Ned. "With your looks, you could be a star."

Ned glanced at Nancy, his ears red with embarrassment. "Well, I don't know . . ."

"And you read so well today," Laura gushed. "You have talent, I'm sure of it."

Ned stared at his plate. "Not really."

"Oh, yes! With a little coaching you'd be terrific."

"Um, do you really think so?" His eyes were now fixed on her.

She fluttered her long lashes. "Why, *I* could teach you a lot."

That's it! Nancy thought. She folded her napkin and placed it on the table with care. She'd rather have wadded it into a ball and thrown it at Laura. Or Ned. Or both.

Focus on the case, Nancy told herself. She glanced at George, who was listening to Matt describe the fuss the hospital staff had made over him once they recognized him as Brent from "Ventura Boulevard."

Never mind, Nancy thought, I can handle this on my own. She stood up and went over to Evelyn, whispering into her ear. "I need to talk to you, if you don't mind."

"Of course, dear." Evelyn pushed aside her chocolate cake. "Let's go over to my house. I don't want to be tempted by all these heavenly calories, anyway."

Nancy saw that Ned was watching her as they began to leave. He started to get up, but Laura grabbed his arm and whispered something in his ear. He flashed Nancy an apologetic smile, shrugged his shoulders helplessly, and sat back down again.

Nancy jerked open the door, annoyed. The night air was crisp, and the blanket of snow muffled all sound. She led Evelyn to the two dark cars, and the director identified them. One belonged to her, the other to Joseph Brunner.

Nancy decided to ask Ned to talk to the playwright. She had to find out if he was familiar with the Barn's word-processing program. She also wanted him to open up on who he thought might be trying to sabotage his play. Plus, it would take Ned away from Laura for a while.

A few minutes later, in Evelyn's cozy living room, Nancy told her about Fiona's mother.

Evelyn was surprised. "My goodness, I had no idea Fiona was related to Shannon Sweeney. She's never said a word."

"Maybe she's ashamed of her mother." Nancy watched the lights twinkling on Evelyn's Christmas tree.

"I doubt it. Shannon is no worse than a lot of actresses I could name. I've worked with her several times, and I can tell you, she's not nearly as wicked as the character in Joseph's play."

Evelyn tucked her legs under her on the couch. "No, I think Fiona kept the relationship secret because she wants to become a success on her own, not as the daughter of a famous movie star. Fiona's proud."

"She's also the only person in the compound who has a motive—that we know about—for not wanting the play to open. Do you think she's desperate enough to try arson?"

"Fiona? Never! She loves the Barn as much as I do. Now, I wish you'd stop talking about arson. Those notes were just a mean joke."

Rather than argue with the director, Nancy

decided to play along with her. "Then who is mean enough to do something like that? Joseph Brunner?"

"Well, maybe. But why would he threaten his own play?"

"I don't know—yet. In the meantime Charles Ferguson is the only other person with a known motive. He's determined to own this property, and he strikes me as a ruthless man."

"Surely you can't think that he would stoop to such low tricks." She stood up and walked over to the window. Her lovely face reflected the glow of the Christmas lights. "Besides, how could the man sneak on and off the property without being seen?"

"Perhaps he paid someone in the company to slip the notes into your script."

"But who?"

"I don't know, but I plan to check into it." Nancy crossed her long, slim legs. "Let's concentrate on this afternoon. Joseph owns a dark sedan. Was he in the theater the entire time we were out riding?"

"Yes, well, most of the time. He did leave for a few minutes at one point."

"When?"

"I don't remember. I was too involved to notice."

"Who else left the theater?"

"Well, Jill went to town."

"What about Marla?"

"She was busy setting up the press conference. She contacted every newspaper, radio, and TV station in the state. She's terribly forgetful, but she sure pulled off that press conference."

"Was she working out of the theater office? She could have left for a while, and you wouldn't have known."

"But Howie would. He was in the box office all afternoon, too. Surely you don't think she wrote those notes?"

"I'm just curious about her." Nancy stood up and joined Evelyn at the window. The heavy cloud cover had thinned, and a full moon was peeking out. "How did you two meet?"

"We bumped into each other at auditions in New York. We were the same 'type,' so our agents sent us out for the same roles. Sometimes she won the part, sometimes I did." She laughed. "Most of the time neither of us did."

"So in a way you were rivals."

"Very *friendly* rivals. Look, Nancy, all this is pointless. The danger is over, and I have a play to open—"

"Hello, everyone," Marla said as she came into the room. "Evelyn, have you seen my knitting? I can't find it *anywhere.*"

"Didn't you take it up to your room before dinner?" Evelyn said.

"Ah, that must be it!" Marla turned toward the staircase, then stopped. "Nancy, that young man of yours is gorgeous. I'd keep an eye on him if I were you."

Nancy flushed. So Marla had noticed how Ned and Laura were carrying on. After saying good night, she headed for the Lodge.

Ned and Laura were on the couch next to the fireplace, bent over a photo album, almost cheek to cheek. "That's me in *Romeo and Juliet,*" Laura was saying, pointing to a picture. "And here are the reviews. This critic wrote—"

"Nancy!" Ned said as soon as he saw her. "I wondered where you'd gone."

"I was talking to Evelyn. Can I see you outside for a minute?"

"Sure." Ned handed the album to Laura. "I'll be back in a little while."

"Well, all right—" she said, and pouted.

Ned put on his jacket and followed Nancy out onto the porch.

"What's the problem?" he asked, zipping up his jacket.

Don't get angry, Nancy told herself. Focus on the case. "I need your help," she said, then told him about Joseph's fight with Fiona and the fact that he owned a dark sedan. "I want you to talk to him. Find out if he's familiar with the Barn's computer and ask him where he went when he left the theater today."

"Sure, I'll go talk to him right now." He turned away.

Nancy hesitated, then said, "Wait a minute, Ned, there's something else."

"You sound upset." He came back and put an arm around her shoulder. "What's the matter?"

Anger spilled out in one word: "Laura."

Ned hugged her. "Laura? You don't have to worry about her. She's just being friendly."

"Is that what you call it? Are you blind? She's a flirt. She's the type who has to charm the boots off every man she meets, just to prove how perfectly adorable she is!"

"Well, she does get a little carried away at times," Ned said.

"And you're falling for it!" Nancy countered. "You spend more time with her than you do helping me!"

"Hey, wait a minute, Nan!"

Nancy didn't wait. She pulled away from him and jumped off the porch.

"I was only checking her out as a suspect," he said.

Nancy swung around and said, "Get real, Ned."

Then she ran through the snow, and the darkness enveloped her.

Chapter Eight

"NANCY!" NED CRIED, snow flying as he plowed through the drifts after her. He was tall and strong, but Nancy's long legs quickly carried her up the hill toward the stable as gracefully as a deer.

He caught up to her just as she reached the empty paddock. Hearing his steps closing behind her, she gave up the race and leaned against the fence, her breath coming out in quick, frosty puffs.

He stopped a few feet away. "Nan, I'm sorry. I know how it must seem to you, but really, Laura doesn't mean anything to me. It's just that she's—"

"A beautiful actress who thinks you could be a movie star."

Ned laughed. "Me, in the movies? No thanks. I mean, it's nice that she thinks so."

"Admit it, Ned, you love the attention."

He brushed his dark wavy hair off his forehead. "Yes and no. I mean, it's flattering, but also kind of, well, embarrassing. It's just that she sort of sucks you in, and before you know it—"

"You're caught in her trap."

Ned winced. "Yeah, I guess so."

Nancy stared at him for a long moment. She could understand how he felt, and the last thing she wanted to do was lower herself to Laura's level.

She took a step toward him and held out her hands. "I have a magic potion."

"What do you mean?" He stared at her.

"If I touch you with my magic potion, you will be immune to flirts like Laura from this time forward." She stepped closer and gently ran her hands over his forehead, his eyes, his cheeks, his chin. Then she kissed the tips of her fingers and pressed them to his mouth. "Now you are safe forever more."

He gazed into her eyes, then pulled her close in a fierce hug. "Nan, my Nan," he whispered. "There's no one in the world like you."

At breakfast Nancy watched with amusement as Ned deliberately chose a seat far from Laura.

She leaned forward to speak to him. "I can't believe we're opening tomorrow night! Ned, darling, you *are* going to watch dress rehearsal, aren't you?"

"Yes, I'll be there."

On the way to the Lodge, Ned had told Nancy and George that he had knocked on Joseph Brunner's door the night before, but the playwright refused to let him in. This morning he would try again to gain Brunner's confidence.

"You must all come," Marla gushed. "Liz has created some absolutely stunning gowns for Laura. And wait until you see Matt in his tux. Even in a wheelchair, he'll be gorgeous."

Matt squirmed in his chair.

George spoke up. "I'm looking forward to it."

Nancy knew that George had made little progress in getting Fiona to talk. Still, she was determined to succeed now. The plan was that George and Ned would try to befriend the suspects and keep an eye out for any arson attempts.

As the company was preparing to head for the Barn, Nancy said to the people getting up from her table, "I'll join you in a while. I have some personal business to take care of first."

The few leads she'd had were turning into dead ends and she was hoping a thorough search of the compound would turn up something. Before breakfast, she'd taken Howie aside and questioned him about the previous afternoon when she and George had been out riding. From his vantage point in the box office, he'd seen Brunner leave the theater but swore he'd returned within five minutes. He also said he'd heard Marla in the office talking on the telephone, setting up the press conference. Like Evelyn, he was sure everyone else was in the theater the entire time.

As soon as everyone left, Nancy set out. With Evelyn's permission, she searched her house for kerosene cans or anything that could start another fire. She discovered an almost empty container of paint thinner in Evelyn's basement.

One by one, she searched the outbuildings. There was plenty of paint in the shed where the scenery was built, but it was all latex and not flammable. Next she checked the nearby woods but came across nothing.

She was in one of the girls' cabins, searching the closet, when the door opened.

"Oh, *there* you are!" Marla said. "What are you doing?"

Nancy was relieved that it wasn't one of the crew members who had discovered her poking around where she didn't belong. So far she'd been able to keep her investigation quiet.

"I was searching for anything that might be used to start a fire," Nancy explained.

"Why don't I help you?" Marla said eagerly. "I *had* to get away from the phones for a while. The press is calling from all over the country to ask about Matt's injury. You can only repeat the same information fifty times before you start going bananas. Poor Liz—I've left her to deal with it for a while."

"Thanks," Nancy said. "But I really don't think—"

"I've acted in more detective shows than you can count. I'd just love to help. Now, where shall I start?"

Nancy was forced to accept Marla's assistance. They worked their way through two cabins, finding nothing more exciting than piles of dirty laundry. No hidden cash or any other indication that someone had been bought off by Ferguson. She wasn't disappointed, though, because she genuinely liked the crew and apprentices and didn't want to think that any of them were involved.

They moved on to other cabins. Matt's was neat and tidy, Laura's scattered with clothes and endless jars of makeup. Again they came up with nothing.

In Fiona's homey cabin, the walls were covered with framed movie posters, the bedspread and curtains were a cheerful red print, and a vase of fresh carnations stood on the bureau.

Nancy noticed the edge of a letter sticking out from the blotter on the desk. The letterhead was Shannon Sweeney's. Nancy unfolded the letter and read the elegant handwriting.

> Fiona, dear,
>
> Please don't worry about the play. I can think of at least a dozen other actresses it could be based on. Yes, it uses some of the

information you gave Brunner, but who will know those stories are true? I am not ashamed of falling in love with Jason in Rome. It was a fantastic, romantic time for both of us. Nor am I the only one who got a little carried away in Paris, although I suppose not everyone hijacks a boat on the Seine.

The point is, honey, my escapades have helped my career. Many actresses are talented, but I was noticed. And as you know, that's the name of the game. So please, keep our family's famous Irish temper under control and don't do anything rash. Let the play go on! I will survive it and so will you.

I love you,
Mom

Marla had been reading over Nancy's shoulder. "That Shannon Sweeney! She'll do anything to attract attention. What a ham."

"Do you know her?" Nancy wondered why Fiona was still so furious with Joseph, in spite of this letter. Her anger must be very deep.

"*Know* her?" Marla sounded scornful. "I did a play with her once and had to fight like the devil to keep her from upstaging me."

"Really?" Nancy kept her talking as they moved on to Joseph's cabin.

Joseph's laptop was gone and scripts of *Alias Angel Divine* were piled on the table. Plenty of kindling for a fire, Nancy thought. The bed was unmade, shirts and ties hung from doorknobs, and damp towels had been dropped on the bathroom floor.

"What a slob," Marla pronounced. "You know, this is fun, poking into people's private lives."

They found nothing of interest in the cabin and were about to leave when Nancy decided to check the closet again. In the back of the top shelf, behind a suitcase, was a script she'd noticed earlier. The label on the box said "Rough Draft." Nancy had assumed it was *Angel* but now discovered it was a different play, one titled *The Social Club.*

Nancy pulled down the box, opened it, and read the first page, a summary of the plot. "This seems to be a play about arson." She picked up the script. Beneath it was a jumble of assorted papers. "These look like research notes."

She gave a few to Marla, and they scanned through them. "Joseph Brunner sure has learned a lot about setting fires!" Marla exclaimed.

Chapter Nine

"LOOK AT THIS." Marla handed one of the papers to Nancy. "It explains how to turn a disposable lighter into a firebomb." She hurried to the door. "I'm going to ask him about this right now."

"No, please don't," Nancy said. "Let me handle it."

"All right, I'll tell him that you want to question him." She opened the door.

"Don't say *question.* Just tell him I want to talk to him," Nancy called as Marla hurried off.

Nancy quickly stuffed the notes and script back in the box, returned it to the top shelf of the closet, and replaced the suitcase she'd moved earlier. Then she glanced around to make sure they had left nothing out of place in the cabin.

She hurried outside, but Marla was already out

of sight. Nancy ran down the path to catch up with her.

Without warning she tripped over a root hidden by the snow. Sharp pain jolted her knee as it hit a rock.

"Ouch!" She rubbed her knee. "Marla, wait for me!" she shouted, but heard no answer. She scrambled to her feet and set off, limping.

She was too late. By the time she found Joseph and Marla in the greenroom, the playwright was furious.

"You did *what?"* Brunner's eyes bulged behind his thick glasses. "How *dare* you search my cabin?"

"As I told you, we're conducting an investigation, right, Nancy?" Marla turned as Nancy limped into the room. "What happened to you?"

"I fell. What did you tell him?" Nancy demanded.

"Well . . ." Marla began.

Joseph cut in. "You have a lot of nerve searching my private belongings! You especially had no right to read that script!"

"Evelyn gave me permission—" Nancy began.

"I don't care what Evelyn said! She thinks she's queen of the hive, and she's not! That was *my* writing, *my* creative child, and no one is allowed to see it without *my* permission!"

"Look here, Brunner," Marla said. "We are investigating a serious crime, and we have just proved that you know a great deal about arson."

Nancy groaned.

"I *have* to know about arson, or how could I write a play about it? Research isn't a crime!"

"But setting malicious fires is," Nancy said, giving in to Marla's line of questioning. All the damage was done. "What do you know about the fire here in the greenroom, and the one that burned down the prop shed?"

"Nothing! Are you implying that I—"

Nancy tried to sound reasonable. "We're simply asking—"

"You break into my cabin and then you have the nerve to accuse me of arson?"

"The door wasn't locked," Marla pointed out. "So we didn't break in."

Nancy wished Marla would disappear. She was making the situation worse.

"It's an invasion of privacy!" He pounded his fist on the table. "I hope someone *does* burn down this dirty, drafty old pile of boards! It's just what Evelyn Caldwell deserves!"

He pushed past Marla and stormed out of the room.

Marla grinned, but Nancy shook her head and sighed. Any hope of getting information from Joseph was gone now. Unless Ned could work miracles.

The cast and crew began to file into the greenroom on a break, heading straight for the coffee maker.

Nancy watched as George cornered Fiona. The

technical director seemed tense and irritable, but George did manage to coax a smile from her.

"Ned." Nancy caught him as he came in the door. "Did you find out anything from Joseph this morning? I'm afraid Marla and I—"

"Ned, darling, what do you think of this costume?" Laura, dark curls spilling down her back, appeared at his side. She wore a blue velvet gown, trimmed with lace at the neck and wrists. "I don't like all this itchy lace." She rubbed her slender throat.

He studied the petite actress. "I think you look . . . uh, very nice."

"Excuse me, Laura, but I need to speak to Ned for a moment." Nancy took him by the arm.

"All right," Laura said, frowning. "I wonder if Jill remembered to buy the herbal tea I asked her for." She drifted over to the coffee table after leaving Ned with a charming smile.

Nancy raised her eyebrows at Ned and he chuckled, giving her a brief hug. They went out into the hall, and she told him about the scene with Joseph. Ned reported that the playwright had been too preoccupied with rehearsal for them to talk. They agreed he should try to have lunch with Brunner.

"That's it, everyone," Sherri announced a few minutes later. "Break is over. Places, please. Places for the top of scene three." Cast and crew filed out into the hall, carrying their coffee cups.

Nancy, Ned, and George sat near the back of

the theater. Nancy told George about the search and the encounter with Joseph.

The lights dimmed and rehearsal began.

Laura flitted around the stage, plumping up cushions, adjusting pictures, and rearranging ornaments on the Christmas tree. The doorbell rang, and she opened the door for Matt. He handed her a large, gaily wrapped package.

"Merry Christmas, Angel," Matt said. "Am I forgiven?"

Laura took the package and kissed him on the cheek. "Of course you are, sweetheart. It was a silly fight over nothing."

"I wouldn't exactly call it nothing."

Laura tossed the package on the couch and walked to the front of the stage. "Evelyn, I can't work in this costume. It's too tight across the back and this cheap lace is irritating my skin."

"I'll have Liz fix it at lunchtime," Evelyn said. "Let's take it from the top of the scene. Matt, you're offstage."

The rehearsal continued, but other problems arose. Joseph kept interrupting, objecting to Evelyn's direction. The telephone rang too soon. A desk drawer was stuck. Matt's wheelchair hit a table and knocked it over. Both he and Laura were so rattled they forgot lines they'd always known, and once Matt even jumped into the middle of another scene. Tempers rose with each mistake, but they stumbled through it somehow.

Only Evelyn stayed calm, occasionally reminding them of the old theater maxim: Bad dress rehearsal, good opening. In other words, the worse the rehearsal, the better the performance.

Everyone was glad to break for lunch, except Matt, who said he was too nervous to eat and sat in a chair near the fireplace. George and Fiona sat together at a small table in the dining area of the Lodge. Nancy could see that George's manner was loosening Fiona up.

Joseph asked the cook for a tray to take to his cabin. It was obvious he was still furious about the search.

Naturally Laura chose a seat next to Ned. As the actress bombarded him with questions about her performance, Ned caught Nancy's eye and surreptitiously winked.

Nancy grinned, then concentrated on the case. If Joseph Brunner was the arsonist, why would he want to destroy his own play? She knew he disagreed with the way Evelyn was directing it. Maybe he wanted someone else to produce it instead.

The more Nancy turned the idea over in her mind, the flimsier his motive seemed. If he wanted to, he could take the play somewhere else, couldn't he? She would have to ask Evelyn about his right to withdraw it.

Was there another motive? He obviously didn't have a warm spot in his heart for Evelyn.

Then there was Charles Ferguson. She had to find out more about the businessman.

After the company left the Lodge at the end of lunch, Nancy met briefly with George and Ned. "How is it going with Fiona?" she asked George.

"I didn't find out much more than we already know. She's very close to her mother, and she hates Joseph for betraying her. She keeps saying she'll get even with him, but I think it's just talk. I like her, and I just don't see her setting the Barn on fire. She loves this place."

"Plus, she has alibis for each accident," Nancy commented before turning to Ned. "Would you drive me over to Ferguson's house? I'll use the excuse that we're collecting Evelyn's horses from his barn."

"I'll come, too," George said.

"I need you to stay here and keep an eye on the Barn," Nancy said. "And see if you can find a chance to question Brunner. I'll ride Applause back and lead Bravo."

A short while later Ned drove the rental car into the driveway of the Ferguson mansion and parked by the barn. Through the open door they saw the sedan. The sports car was gone.

"Before we go up to the house," Nancy said, "I want to take another look at that car. It all happened so fast I only got a glimpse of it. But maybe I'll recognize the grille or the headlights."

"You said the engine was warm, and in this weather it would cool quickly. So someone must have been driving it just before you arrived," Ned surmised.

"That's right." Nancy got out and walked to the front of Ferguson's car. She studied it for a couple of minutes but couldn't be sure it was the one. She couldn't rule it out, either.

They went around to the front of the house and knocked at the door. The housekeeper opened it and told them Ferguson was out.

Nancy said she was there to pick up the horses, then added, "While we're here, we wondered if we could take a quick look at Mr. Ferguson's computer. The printer at the Barn is broken," Nancy lied. "Ms. Caldwell wondered if we could borrow this one—only in case of an emergency, of course," she added when she saw the housekeeper frown.

"I don't think Mr. Ferguson would be happy about that," Hilda said, "but I guess it can't hurt to let you take a look."

"He's not too crazy about the Red Barn, is he?" Nancy smiled at her.

Hilda led them into the study. "He's his own man. What he likes, he likes, and what he doesn't —watch out. I served him his beef too rare one night and heard about it for a week after."

Hilda left them alone, and Nancy checked the printer. It was the same brand as the one at the Barn. "The notes could have been printed on this system. Let's boot up the computer and see what program he uses," she suggested.

"Do you think we should?" Ned asked.

"It'll only take a minute." She turned the

computer on and watched the screen. "Oh, boy, I should have guessed. We can't enter the program until we type in the password and—"

"Just what do you think you're doing?"

Nancy whirled around as Charles Ferguson strode into the study, his eyes blazing.

Chapter Ten

NANCY'S HEART RACED so fast she wondered if Ferguson could see it fluttering under her sweater. "M-Mr. Ferguson," she stammered. "You startled us."

"What are you doing with my computer?" Ferguson's hands were balled into fists, and his face was a splotchy red.

"Nothing." Nancy tried to keep the quaver out of her voice. "The printer at the Barn is broken, and we wondered if yours was compatible with our system. While we were looking at it, we noticed that the computer was turned on."

"I never leave it on!"

"Are you sure? When I have to leave mine for a while, I turn down the brightness on the screen. It's better than rebooting it too often."

Ferguson glared at her. "I know that! What kind of fool do you think I am?"

"Are you sure you didn't do that this time? The screen was dark, but I heard the hum." Nancy gave him an innocent smile. "I have to confess, I was also curious. I'm thinking of upgrading my system, and your computer is one of the ones I'm considering, so I turned up the brightness to take a tiny peek. I'm really sorry. I hope you don't mind."

Ferguson reached past her and switched the machine off. "I do mind. What are you doing poking around in my office?"

Nancy edged toward the door, followed by Ned. "We really came over to collect Ms. Caldwell's horses. It was good of you to take care of them."

At the mention of the horses, Ferguson's face softened a little. "Fine animals, especially that big bay gelding. Is he for sale?"

"I don't think so, but I'll tell Ms. Caldwell you're interested." Her heart rate slowed to normal, now that Ferguson apparently had accepted her story.

"Tell her to name her price. And while you're about it, tell her she'd better reconsider my offer on her property. The terms are not only fair, but very generous, and she'd be smart to accept it before it's too late."

"What does that mean?" Nancy asked.

He gave her a sharp glance. "Never mind. Just

give her my message. And now I assume you want to collect your horses."

"Yes. Thanks again for taking care of them."

His only answer was a brief nod.

Nancy was glad to escape to the barn. While Ned helped her saddle the mare, he said firmly, "I don't want you riding across country. Take the road home, and I'll follow you."

"But it's shorter to go over the fields."

"It doesn't matter. Ferguson is a ruthless man. I don't want you roaming around on your own any more."

"Ned, you know I can take care of myself."

He hugged her. "You're my girl, and I don't want anything to happen to you."

Nancy snuggled in his arms. "Okay, the road it is. Just promise me that when Laura starts her cute little act again, you'll remember what you just said."

"You're my girl," he repeated. He kissed the tip of her nose.

Nancy enjoyed the ride back on Applause, but Bravo didn't like trailing the mare. He was used to leading, and he insisted on cantering beside them all the way back.

After they'd turned the horses loose in their own paddock, Nancy stopped at Evelyn's house to use the phone.

"I'm going to call my father to ask him to run a check on Ferguson. I want to know about his business background."

"Good idea. I'll meet you in the theater."

Evelyn had given Nancy permission to use her phone whenever she needed to. She went into the living room. When she dialed her father's office, she was immediately put through to Carson Drew.

"Nancy! I'm glad you called. How are you doing?"

"Just fine, Dad, but I haven't solved the case yet. I need some information." She told him about Ferguson. "And also, could you try to find out if a playwright named Joseph Brunner has any kind of criminal record? He's my other major suspect."

They chatted about Christmas plans for a while, then Nancy sent her love to Hannah, the housekeeper who had been with the family since Nancy was three years old. When she hung up the phone, she realized that Marla was standing in the doorway. How long had she been standing there?

"Hi! Don't mind me," Marla said. "I came back to find my knitting. Have you seen it anywhere?"

Nancy pointed to a needlepoint bag on a chair. "Is that it?"

"Why, yes. Silly me, I was searching for it all over the theater. Was that your father on the phone?" Marla rummaged through her bag and pulled out a ball of yarn.

"Yes," Nancy said simply, wondering how

much of her conversation Marla had overheard. After her disastrous mishandling of Joseph, Nancy was not eager to have her "help" again.

"Do you think Evelyn will like this color? I'm knitting her a scarf for Christmas, but I wonder if this shade is too green."

"Well, it *is* bright," Nancy said, "but it should look good on Evelyn."

"That's what I thought at first. Then I thought, no, then I changed my mind again. Oh, well, if she doesn't like it, she doesn't have to wear it. Why are Ferguson and Brunner your main suspects?"

Nancy was startled by the sudden change of subject. "Did—did I say that?"

"You certainly did, and I think you're on the right track. *Definitely.* Someone pointed Charles Ferguson out to me in town the other day, and I could tell right away he's a dangerous man. He reminds me of that director, the one who did that picture in Spain. Oh, what *is* his name? Anyway, he has the same cold eyes and those tight, thin lips. Never trust anyone with thin lips, my dear. I should know." She nodded wisely.

Nancy smiled. "All right. How's rehearsal going?"

"Fine. Now, as to your other suspect, Brunner, I don't like him either. Heaven knows, the theater world is riddled with egotists, but he really takes the cake. Evelyn is directing this play brilliantly, and all he does is complain. It wouldn't surprise me a bit if he's the one who set those fires and sent those notes."

"Then why doesn't he take the play somewhere else?" Nancy asked.

"He can't. Evelyn has a contract giving her exclusive rights. He was happy enough to sign it, and more than happy to take her big, fat check. But now all he does is whine. He's really a pathetic little man."

"That's very interesting. Well, we should be getting back." Nancy moved to the door.

"Wait, my dear. There are two more suspects I don't think you've considered. Fiona Sweeney is one of them."

"I think we've about eliminated her. She has solid alibis for each accident."

"Well, there's one person who I don't think has even occurred to you."

"Who?" Nancy asked.

Marla lowered her voice and glanced at the door. "Evelyn. I know she's my friend and I shouldn't even think of it, but a good detective can't let personal feelings get in the way of solving a crime."

Nancy blinked in surprise. "But why would Evelyn want to burn down her own theater?"

"Have you considered the insurance angle? You know she's having money problems. A nice big chunk of cash from the insurance company would fix that. Then she could sell the property to Ferguson and she'd be rolling in dough."

"I don't know," Nancy said. "I don't think she would have asked me to investigate if she was trying to destroy the Red Barn."

Marla stuffed the yarn back in her bag. "You're probably right. It was just an idea. Well, are you coming or not? I have to finish the display in the lobby."

They walked over to the Barn, and Nancy left Marla in the lobby before joining Ned and George in the back of the theater. Above them, Ben was on the catwalk behind their row, adjusting lights with a huge wrench.

"What do you think of this idea?" Nancy whispered to her friends. "Marla suggested that Evelyn herself might be behind the threats."

"That's ridiculous!" George hissed, angry.

"I agree," Ned said. "What possible motive could she have?"

Nancy explained Marla's insurance theory.

George was so mad she was ready to explode. "Aunt Evelyn would never—"

Just then Ned reached over and shoved Nancy out of her seat!

Chapter Eleven

A SECOND LATER Ned was kneeling at her side. "I'm sorry, Nan. Are you all right?" He touched her face.

"Yes, I'm fine." Her heart was pounding from the sudden surge of adrenaline. "What happened? Why did you shove me?"

"I was looking up when I saw this start to fall." Ned showed her a heavy stainless steel wrench a foot and a half long that he picked up from the chair where she'd been sitting. Nancy raised her eyes to the catwalk, where Ben stood, frozen.

"Did you drop this, Ben?" she asked, standing up.

"No, I didn't, I swear. I still have my wrench right here. See?" He held it up.

"Did you leave another one on the edge of the

catwalk?" Evelyn asked as she and everyone else walked toward Nancy.

"No!" Ben protested. "I wouldn't do that." His voice was shaking.

"Did any of you leave this wrench up there?" Evelyn asked the crew.

They all shook their heads, shocked into silence.

"Come on, someone admit to it," Evelyn said. "It was an accident, and fortunately no one got hurt. If you made a mistake, no one will blame you. It's important that we know."

Fiona and Marla pushed through the lobby doors. "What's going on?" Fiona asked. "We heard yelling."

Nancy explained, then asked Fiona, "Where were you when this happened?"

"In the office, on the phone, ordering replacement lamps for the Fresnels. Two bulbs blew this morning."

"And, darling, I was right out in the lobby doing the display," Marla offered.

Nancy counted the group. "Where's Joseph?"

"Right here." He walked out onstage from the wings. "I was getting a cup of coffee. What happened?"

"Someone apparently left this wrench on the edge of the catwalk," Evelyn explained. "It fell and almost hit Nancy."

"She doesn't look hurt," Joseph said gruffly.

"No, thank goodness. You really are all right, aren't you?" Evelyn asked her.

"I'm perfectly fine," Nancy repeated.

"I'm so glad." Evelyn glanced at her watch. "All right, everyone, back to work. We'll get to the bottom of this later. Right now we have to finish the last scene. It's nearly dinnertime."

While the crew scattered to their posts, Nancy talked to Ned. "How did you happen to see the wrench?"

"I heard Ben and glanced up at him. It was then I saw the gleam of something falling. Sorry about shoving you. No, actually I'm not, 'cause you're still here." He circled her in a giant bear hug, which Nancy gratefully returned.

"Was it coming from the catwalk?" she asked, still in his arms.

He remained silent for a moment. "Come to think of it, it was higher up than that, maybe up in the rafters."

The Barn's antique wooden beams were exposed, like the ribs of a skeleton. Apparently once there had been a hayloft, but it had been removed. In its place was the catwalk Ben was working on. It was a narrow balcony that stretched across the back of the theater. A narrow metal ladder on the rear wall led up to it.

"Did you see anyone up there any place except Ben?" Nancy asked.

"No," Ned said. "And, come to think of it, he was working about five feet behind us."

"Places, please." Evelyn clapped her hands. "Let's take it from Laura's entrance. Come on, places. Don't forget, we open tomorrow night."

Nancy was itching to investigate the rafters but knew she'd have to wait. She couldn't disturb rehearsal, and she didn't want to upset the cast and crew. It was better to let everyone think the wrench had fallen by accident.

The excited talk at dinner was only about the play. The replacement Christmas trees had been decorated, the last of the fake presents wrapped, and Fiona had finally tracked down a set of identical holly plates.

"I know it's crazy to be so nervous about my lines," Matt admitted to George and Nancy as he helped himself to a chicken drumstick. "I really know every word in the script, but during rehearsal I keep going blank."

"Stage fright must be really scary," George said.

"It's the worst! The only way I can fight it is to go over the script again and again and again." He flashed his famous Brent smile at George. "I was wondering if you'd be willing to cue me after dinner?"

George blushed. "You want me to read the play with you?"

"If you don't have any other plans."

"Oh, no. I don't! I'd love to!" She turned to Nancy. "Unless . . ."

Nancy made a quick decision. She had planned to ask George help her check out the Barn, but she couldn't deny her friend a chance to rehearse with Matt. She smiled. "I don't have any plans."

She turned to her left to find Ned deep in conversation with Laura. Nancy couldn't help herself.

"Ned, darling," she said, imitating Laura. "I need to talk to you right after dinner."

He started chuckling, then caught himself and just said, "Sure."

As soon as coffee was served, Nancy asked Ned and Evelyn to join her by the fire. They kept their voices low so they wouldn't be overheard by the others at the tables. Everyone was giddy with preopening excitement, and the room buzzed with conversation.

"Evelyn, I'm very concerned," Nancy began. "I still haven't found out who wrote those arson threats, and opening night is tomorrow."

"But, dear, we decided not to worry about that anymore. Why don't you relax and enjoy your visit, as George is doing?" She nodded at George, who was laughing at something Matt had said.

"Evelyn, I don't believe the danger is over. I'm going to find out who sent those notes and set those fires, but if I haven't solved this case by tomorrow night, you have to take some precautions."

"Goodness, you're persistent. Why are you so convinced we still have a problem?"

"Someone is trying to stop my investigation. I'm positive that falling wrench was planned. Why else did it land on the seat where I always sit to watch rehearsal?"

"Oh, dear, you don't really think so, do you? That would be terrible." She rubbed the back of her neck, then smiled. "Well, if you're right, I'm sure you'll find out who it is."

"Yes, I will," Nancy said. "But I still want you to hire extra guards for tomorrow night. Also, we should have plenty of fire extinguishers on hand. Just in case."

Evelyn sighed. "More money. Do you really think it's necessary?"

"Yes, I do."

"Oh, well, if you insist. Now, if you'll excuse me, I must talk to Joseph about Laura's monologue in scene four."

Ned and Nancy walked over to the Red Barn. The air inside was chilly, and the deserted theater felt hollow. Their hushed voices and footsteps sounded too loud as they echoed in the gloomy stillness.

Ned and Nancy turned on the lights and also got flashlights from the office. Then they climbed up the ladder to the catwalk, sweeping their flashlights over the rafters. "We're not up high enough," Nancy said. "We can't see from here."

"Let's get the scaffold," Ned suggested.

They found it stored behind the rear stage curtain and rolled the tall iron structure down the ramp into the auditorium. "Jerry had moved this into the auditorium yesterday after rehearsal, just before the press conference." Ned grunted as they wheeled the heavy scaffold up the aisle. "I don't know how he managed it all by himself."

"Wait a minute." Nancy stopped and brushed a stray curl off her forehead. "Did you mean the scaffold was left in the back of the theater last night? That means anyone could have climbed up with the wrench."

"You're right. I didn't remember it until just now."

"Hurry up, let's get it in place. I can't wait to see what's up there."

A couple of minutes later, Nancy scrambled up the iron bars. Ned stayed below to steady the structure. Once on the scaffold's platform, she found she could reach up and touch the beam over her head.

Her flashlight revealed a lacy network of cobwebs. "Am I pointing my light directly over the seat?" she called down to Ned.

"A little more to your right," he called up to her.

The flashlight played over the rough timbers. A section about two feet long on the bottom rafter was slightly wider than the rest of the beam. Nancy reached up and ran her hand over the wood. A thin board had been attached to the side of the beam. She found hinges at the top of the board and a hook at the bottom. A length of transparent fish line was tied to the hook. With her flashlight she traced the line as it passed through a series of hooks running along the rafter to the side wall.

"I found it!" Nancy shouted. "Wow, someone went to a lot of trouble."

She stretched up and pulled on the line until the board swung up on its hinges to make a right angle with the rafter and held. Now it formed a shelf just the right size to hold the big wrench. She released the line, and the board dropped. Any object lying on the shelf—such as a wrench—would fall straight down onto her seat.

Nancy described the contraption to Ned, then scrambled down. "Let's find out where the line leads."

They hurried over to the wall and finally spotted the transparent line. It dangled down from the rafters and stopped a couple of feet over their heads.

"Someone cut it," Ned said, disappointed.

"But it must have run through more hooks. We should be able to find them." They searched all along the wall but found no trace. The hooks must have been removed. The wall was made of rough board, scraped, scarred, and pitted with more than a hundred years of use. They couldn't even find holes left by the hooks.

Nancy spoke slowly. "Ned, we knew it before, but now it really hits me. We are looking for someone who is extremely clever. Someone who is very determined. I'm beginning to wonder if we'll be able to catch this someone before opening night. If we don't, when the curtain goes up tomorrow, it really might be in flames."

Chapter Twelve

NANCY TOSSED AND TURNED all night, dreaming about fires. At breakfast she watched the logs burning in the Lodge's cozy hearth and saw in her mind's eye the Barn blazing out of control. The thought terrified her.

The day passed in a flurry of activity. The excitement of the night before had turned to panic as everyone scurried to take care of a hundred and one details. There was so much to be done and so little time to do it that Nancy and her friends found themselves caught up in the production.

Evelyn had scheduled a full run-through of the play for the morning and again for the afternoon. Nancy thought "stumble-through" would have been a better description for both rehearsals.

Matt dropped line after line and insisted that

George work with him during every break. One of Laura's costumes suddenly didn't fit, and Liz had to alter it twice before the actress was satisfied.

Then three more lights blew, and Fiona had to send Howie all the way to New Haven to get more because the replacement shipment hadn't arrived. Nancy was asked to fill in for him at the box office. The phone rang constantly, although the play was sold out for the entire run.

The couch for scene five hadn't been delivered, so Ned helped Jerry and Ben carry over the one from Evelyn's living room.

Joseph was impossible through it all. He was all over the theater, raging at one scene, praising another, fretting about the set, the lights, the costumes, shouting at Evelyn, the cast, and especially the crew.

Ned reported that he'd caught him in the greenroom and tried to find out if he knew the Barn's word-processing program. Joseph had just stared at Ned as if he'd come from Mars, then stalked off.

Nancy became more and more frustrated as the day flew by. Everyone was so busy and nerves were so ragged that she had little hope of pinning down the arsonist. That day nothing in the world existed except *Alias Angel Divine.*

The only solid information Nancy managed to get came from her father. When she called him, late in the day, he reported that Charles Ferguson had a reputation as a tough, shrewd businessman but had never been suspected of illegal activities. However, he had bought out two companies that had been destroyed by suspicious fires.

"He picked up a place called Medford Mills for a song two years ago," Carson explained. "A fire had gutted the building, but the brick exterior was solid. He threw a few million dollars into it, turned it into a classy condominium with shops and restaurants, and has already made back his investment."

"Wow," Nancy said.

"He did the same thing with an old factory in Rhode Island twelve years ago and has made a fortune ten times over with it."

"Was either fire proved to be arson?"

"No. But even if it was, that doesn't mean he was behind it."

"Thanks, Dad." Nancy was quiet for a moment. "What about Joseph Brunner? Anything suspicious in his background?"

"Nothing except a lawsuit by a lady who claimed he based his first Broadway hit on some confidential information she gave him," Carson Drew replied.

"Did she win the case?"

"No, he did. And of course the scandal helped sell more tickets, making it an even bigger hit."

"It doesn't seem fair, does it?" Nancy said.

"Not to me, it doesn't."

They spoke a few more minutes, then Nancy headed over to the Lodge.

Matt didn't come to dinner. He and George were holed up in his cabin, going over lines. George was so worried about him that she said she couldn't eat.

Nancy's anxiety grew as she donned a stylish black miniskirt, tights, pumps, and a blue silk tunic for the opening. She couldn't remember when she'd been so frustrated by a case. She tried to tell herself that if a fire did break out, they were well prepared for it.

George and Ned, plus two security guards, would be backstage during the performance. Four other guards, dressed as members of the audience, would mingle with the crowd. Fire extinguishers stood ready in every corner of the theater.

As Nancy made her way to the theater, she noticed that the parking lot was already filling up and the audience was streaming into the Barn. Just then she saw a silver sports car screech to a halt in front of Evelyn's house. Charles Ferguson got out, ran up the front steps, and pounded on the door.

Nancy went inside the theater and found Evelyn and Marla in the lobby. "You have a visitor," she told the director.

The three of them hurried over to the house.

Ferguson was pacing up and down the porch, scowling.

"May I help you?" Evelyn said.

Ferguson wheeled around and stared at her. "You're Evelyn Caldwell." It sounded like an accusation.

"How do you do, Mr. Ferguson." She held out her hand.

He ignored it. His eyes didn't leave her face. "I've come to double my offer."

"Double it?" Evelyn laughed. "Thank you, anyway, but I have no plans to sell the Barn."

"You have to sell. If you don't, I'll go to the zoning board and make them listen to me," he said.

"I think you'll find my permits are in order and that the town fully backs this theater. We generate a lot of profit for local restaurants and businesses."

"Look at all this traffic! And noise! I won't stand for it!"

"It will quiet down once the curtain goes up," Evelyn assured him.

"And start up all over again as soon as I go to bed!" he fired back at her.

Evelyn raised her eyebrows at him. "You go to bed at ten o'clock on Friday nights?"

For a minute it seemed as if she'd bested him, but then he shook himself out of his daze. "I'm not here to discuss my sleeping habits. Name your price and I'll meet it. This theater has to go!"

Evelyn gave him a lovely smile. "Have you ever seen a play, Mr. Ferguson?"

"Of course I have," he blurted out. "On Broadway. That's where theaters belong, not in my backyard."

"Would you like to see the play tonight?" she asked with delight. "I can guarantee you'll be in bed by ten-thirty at the latest. I'd be happy to give you a complimentary ticket."

He froze, his eyes still fixed on Evelyn's beautiful face. "You were in *A Stranger Calls,* weren't you?"

"Yes. That was one of the first movies I made. Did you like it?"

He gulped. "You were the woman on the train."

"Yes."

"You wore a black veil," he went on.

"Yes, I did. I hate to change the subject, but it's almost curtain time. Would you like to stay to see the play this evening?"

He started shaking his head, as if the fact that he was talking to *the* Evelyn Caldwell was only just sinking in.

"Is that a yes?" Evelyn's smile became dazzling.

"Yes. I said yes." He bit off the words.

"Then come with me." She linked her arm through his, and they strolled over to the theater.

Marla looked at Nancy and said, "They don't call her the Lion Tamer for nothing."

"What do you mean?" Nancy asked.

"The fiercest man turns into a pussycat when she's around." Marla was only half joking.

Nancy glanced at her watch. Only a few minutes to curtain. "I have to check with the guards again." She started for the Barn.

"Surely you don't think all these precautions are necessary, do you? I mean, isn't it a bit much?" Marla hurried to keep up with her.

"Not when lives may be at stake," Nancy said.

"My goodness, what a worrywart you are. I agree with Evelyn. As much as I dislike Joseph and Ferguson, I've decided the whole thing is just a ridiculous joke. No one would actually set fire to a theater with over two hundred people in it."

"I hope you're right." Nancy left Marla in the lobby and checked in with the guards. She whispered to the one closest to Ferguson, pointing him out. The guard would follow him throughout the evening. Another one had been assigned to Joseph, who was pacing up and down at the rear of the house.

When Nancy went around to the stage door, she found the backstage in chaos.

Matt was trembling so hard his wheelchair shook. George sat next to him, murmuring encouragement. Laura flitted between dressing room and greenroom, fishing for compliments from Ned every two seconds. Sherri was having problems with the headset that connected her to the lighting booth. Both security guards said everything was fine.

"Good lu—" Nancy began to say as she left.

"No! No!" Laura snapped. "Never say that! The theater ghost will hear you, and heaven knows what disasters will follow."

"Right, I forgot," Nancy said. "Break a leg."

"Thank you, darling. Ned, do you *really* think this hairstyle is flattering?"

Ned tossed Nancy a look of helpless frustration. She covered her mouth with her hand, hiding a giggle, and left.

She hurried back to the lobby and saw the ushers, the two apprentices, closing the doors behind the last few people entering the theater. They then went backstage to help with scene changes.

Nancy heard the opening music begin and was about to go into the theater when she smelled something.

Smoke!

Chapter Thirteen

NANCY PEERED down the hallway off the lobby. The men's room door was ajar, and a wisp of smoke was creeping out.

Should she call the guards? The fuss and commotion would disrupt the play. No, she'd investigate first.

Grabbing a fire extinguisher, she ran down the hall. The tall metal wastebasket just inside the door was in flames. Nancy directed a stream of foam at it. The fire was quickly smothered, and in less than a minute all that remained was a wet, smoky mess.

Nancy turned on the ventilation fan and opened the window. Piece by piece, she sorted through the soggy paper towels. Halfway down, she came across the remains of a cigarette filter.

Had someone tossed a lighted cigarette into the wastebasket? By accident? Or on purpose?

There was no way to be certain. Briefly Nancy thought of calling the police, but what could they do? And Evelyn would be furious.

She placed the wet towels back in the can, took it down the hall to the utility closet, and covered it with a plastic garbage bag. The evidence would be safe there in case it was needed later.

She found an empty wastebasket and put it in the men's room, which was almost aired out by now. By intermission no one would guess that a fire had been started in there.

Posting one of the security guards in the lobby, she went into the theater. Once her eyes adjusted to the dark, she spotted Evelyn, Ferguson, and Marla sitting in the last row. Joseph stood against the back wall in the corner.

Nancy studied the playwright. It didn't take a vast knowledge of arson to toss a lighted cigarette into a can full of paper towels. But with the security guard following his every move, would he have had the opportunity? She'd check with the guard at intermission.

Joseph Brunner was not a pleasant person, but would he stoop to arson with a theater full of people? If so, what would his motive be? If tonight's performance was a success, maybe he'd relax so that she, or Ned, could get him to talk.

Charles Ferguson, though, had a strong motive, and he'd had the opportunity to start the fire.

Nancy planned to ask Evelyn whether she'd been with him all the time before he'd taken his seat and been assigned a security guard by Nancy.

A burst of laughter from the audience made Nancy focus on the stage. It was the scene where Matt tried to teach Angel how to cook a turkey dinner. Nancy had thought it was funny the first time she'd seen it, and now, with the audience, she began to enjoy the play again.

Laura was not only good in the part, she was brilliant. She floated around the stage as if in her own home, beautiful, selfish, dangerous, completely the Angel Divine.

Matt was incredibly elegant, even in a wheelchair. Most surprising of all, he spoke the dialogue as if he'd never dropped a line in his life. Nancy watched him glide through sections that had always given him trouble. George must be relieved, Nancy thought.

Nancy became more and more involved in the play. It moved along so quickly compared to rehearsals that she was surprised when the act ended and the lights went up for intermission. The applause was enthusiastic.

Evelyn was practically dancing on air during intermission as theater patrons heaped praise on the play and on her direction. Nancy caught her alone for a second and whispered a quick question in her ear.

"Yes, Charles went into the men's room before the play." Evelyn spotted someone over Nancy's shoulder. "Janice! How wonderful of you to come! Nancy, this is my friend Janice Johnson. Janice is what we in the theater call an angel."

Nancy shook a hand that glittered with rings. "Hello," she said, smiling. "I don't believe I've ever met an angel before."

The lady laughed. "That's what they call those of us who are foolish enough to invest money in plays. And, Evelyn, you'll think I'm particularly angelic tonight, because I think this play shows a lot of promise. If the second act holds up, I just might consider backing it in New York."

"Terrific!" Evelyn glowed. "I know you won't be disappointed. The second act is even stronger than the first."

Nancy slipped away. It wasn't the right time to tell Evelyn about the fire.

She found the guard assigned to Joseph, and he swore he hadn't let him out of sight for an instant. Yes, Brunner had smoked a cigarette but only outside the Barn.

By the time she checked with the other guards, intermission was over. Nancy went into the theater and was soon caught up in the play again.

When the curtain came down, the applause was thunderous. The audience demanded one curtain call after another. Finally the curtain was lowered for the last time. Excitement was in the air as people began to drift out into the night.

Nancy made her way backstage, where the cast and crew crowded together, celebrating.

"They loved it! They loved me!" Laura cried, dancing around, still in costume.

Matt sat in his wheelchair, beaming, while he accepted congratulations. "It was only nerves, as Evelyn predicted. Once I got out there and felt the audience, well—all I can say is the magic happened." He shook his head, grinning. "What a feeling."

He was holding George's hand. Now he squeezed it and gave her an adoring look. "You helped make it possible."

George was enormously pleased and terribly embarrassed. She didn't say a word, but her joy was clear. Nancy caught Ned's eye across the room. His eyebrows went up, and she knew he'd noticed, too.

Fiona took Nancy aside. "I listened to the comments in the lobby. Everyone knows Joseph bases his characters on real people, and they were all guessing who Angel was. Not one person mentioned my mother!"

"I'm so glad," Nancy said. "Are you going to forgive Joseph now?"

"No way. He told me he's going to make me pay for a new laptop computer. Once a skunk, always a skunk," she proclaimed.

Just then Evelyn arrived. "Charles Ferguson loved the play," she told Nancy. "He wouldn't admit it, of course, but I could tell."

"Hurry up, everyone," Fiona called. "Set up the stage for tomorrow's performance, then let's head for the Lodge. The reviews should be on TV pretty soon."

Soon everyone was scurrying around hanging up costumes, resetting props, collecting discarded programs, and folding up the seats. In a half hour they finished and gathered in the Lodge around the big-screen TV. Nancy found herself caught up in the tension. Would the reviews be good?

She had noticed that several men and women had rushed up the aisle as soon as the curtain came down. Now she realized that these were local television critics, hurrying to meet their deadlines. The reviews were vital. They could make or break Evelyn's chances of taking *Alias Angel Divine* to Broadway.

The first TV station to carry a review was Channel 30. "Matt Duncan has proved he's far more than a handsome face," the critic said. "And Laura James gave the performance of her life."

Cheers went up and they switched the TV to Channel 8, where the reviewer was just launching in. "A bold new play, both hilarious and thought-provoking. . . . Extraordinary performances by two highly talented actors whose stars will be rising," he claimed.

More cheers rang out, followed by yet another review on Channel 3. This one was entirely devoted to Evelyn's direction, saying it showed a true understanding of the quirky but engaging characters and deepest meanings of the play.

The Lodge erupted in joyful shouts, hugs and kisses, slaps on the back, pure delight. Nancy looked around at the happy crowd. No one knew that the Barn had almost burned down, Nancy thought.

Now that they'd made it safely through opening night, did that mean the arsonist would give up? Or was he just waiting for another chance to strike?

Chapter Fourteen

THE PARTY BEGAN. Fiona turned on the CD player, and music filled the air. Tables were pushed back to make room for dancing, and the cook brought out chips, dip, cheese and crackers, and a huge pot of mulled cider.

The cast and crew had friends in the audience who were invited to join the celebration, swelling the group to more than forty people. The noise level rose, and the floor bounced to the beat of dancing feet.

Nancy watched the fun for a while before she forced herself to take Evelyn, Ned, and George out to the kitchen. She told them about the fire.

"Nancy, dear, I'm so grateful you discovered it in time." Evelyn put her hand on Nancy's arm. "But you don't think it was arson, do you? Someone probably thought the cigarette was out and tossed it away, not realizing it was still smoldering."

"Possibly, but, Evelyn—"

"Don't you realize? This play is a hit! There's a good chance it's going to Broadway! Janice is definitely interested in backing it. This is one of the happiest nights of my life. Now, don't worry so much. Come back and join the party!"

"In a minute." Nancy watched her push through the swinging doors. "I wish she'd take off those blinders, or rose-colored glasses—whatever you want to call them."

"Nan, you've got to realize that it takes incredible energy and concentration to put on a play," George said. "Aunt Evelyn has focused on it for weeks—months. Nothing else exists for her right now."

"Okay, but *I've* got to focus on this investigation. We still don't know who the arsonist is."

"Opening night is now over, and the curtain didn't go up in flames, thanks to you," Ned said. "And now it looks like Joseph is ruled out as a suspect. He's out there beaming. He obviously didn't want to sabotage his own show."

"*Someone* is guilty. We can't let down our guard," Nancy said, folding her arms in front of her.

The kitchen doors swung open, and Laura swept in. "Ned, darling, they're playing our song."

"Since when is 'Jingle Bell Rock' your song, Ned?" Nancy asked, trying to smother a laugh.

Laura narrowed her eyes. "Nancy, darling, it's just an expression." She took Ned's hand and dragged him away.

As he went through the door, Ned threw Nancy a here-she-goes-again expression.

"Come on," George said. "You need to forget you're a detective for a while. Let's go have some fun."

"I guess you're right. Anyway, I'll need to rescue Ned soon. He's had a little too much of Laura tonight."

They returned to the party, and Nancy danced with Jerry, then Ben, and then Howie. Finally she cut in on Laura and Ned.

Nancy expected Laura to object. Instead the actress glanced at the door and let out a shriek. "Lars! You came!" She ran across the room, her arms outstretched.

A tall, blond, bearded man literally swept Laura off the floor, spinning her around and around. From that moment on, Laura never left his side. Occasionally Ned and Nancy would glance at them snuggled up together and break out in laughter.

The party grew louder. Nancy, Ned, and George joined a group playing a hilarious game of Truth or Dare, where the rules changed every few minutes. A conga line started up, and they joined in for some silly, old-fashioned fun. They agreed that the highlight of the evening was when Joseph put a Christmas wreath on his head and danced a jig.

Much later Nancy went to get a soda and discovered that the ice bucket was empty. She took it out to the kitchen to refill it and found Marla, Ben, Liz, and a couple of their friends playing a game of poker. From the pile of matchsticks in front of Marla, it was obvious who was winning.

"Come on, guys, ante up." Marla dealt a new hand, the cards flying from her swift fingers. "Five card stud, jokers and threes wild."

"Not again." Ben groaned. "You're killing us."

"Are you a man or a mouse?" Marla grinned.

Nancy paused to watch for a while. Marla seemed to remember every card that had been played, and she was an expert bluffer. She raked in one pile of matchsticks with only a pair of fives in her hand. Liz had folded with two queens.

Was this the same lady who constantly misplaced her glasses and knitting and could never remember a name? Nancy watched as Marla made one lightning-fast decision after another. Now she was seeing the person who had run a theater for a number of years.

It struck Nancy then that she'd overlooked Marla as a suspect, partly because she was Evelyn's good friend. It had hardly been friendly of Marla to suggest that Evelyn might be the arsonist, though.

She needed to find out more about Marla, and right away.

Nancy took the ice bucket back to the table. George and Ned were talking to some of Fiona's friends from New York, and she didn't want to interrupt them. She grabbed her jacket and walked over to Evelyn's house.

Upstairs in Marla's room she found clothes and makeup scattered on every surface. And Marla had gloated over the mess in Joseph's cabin!

Nancy found what she was looking for in a suitcase in the back of the closet: a thick, worn, leather-covered album. It was bulging with newspaper clippings. The first pages dated back to Marla's high school days, then the datelines changed to New York City newspapers.

She replaced the suitcase, turned out the lights, and took the album down to the living room, ready to hide if Marla returned.

She began to read, first about the actress's leading roles in high school, then about bit parts she'd played in off-off-Broadway plays. Slowly the parts got larger, until finally one headline proclaimed: "Marla Kramer to Star at Shubert Theater." Next came another, dated a few days later. "Kramer Seriously Ill, Replaced by Caldwell," it said. Two pictures accompanied the article, one of a young and beautiful Marla, the other of an equally young and lovely Evelyn.

What a shame, Nancy thought. Marla's big

break, her chance to be a star, and then she gets sick. And who takes over the part? Her friend Evelyn. That must have hurt.

Nancy read on and found an interview written after the show had opened. It was titled: "Kramer Says to Caldwell, 'Break a Leg.' " Marla was quoted, congratulating Evelyn on her success and wishing her all the best. " 'It will be my turn next,' the plucky actress told this reporter from her hospital bed."

The rest of the clippings told another story. It was many years before Marla turned into a success—years of supporting roles off Broadway, leads in touring companies performing in places like Milwaukee and Omaha and Tulsa, a few television commercials, and finally minor roles in several TV series and in movies.

The clippings from the last ten years were mostly about Marla's Popcorn Playhouse in Carmel. It had apparently struggled along, producing a hit now and then, an occasional flop, and getting lots of so-so reviews. But whenever Marla performed or directed, the critics praised her talent.

A large envelope was taped to the inside back cover of the album. Nancy pulled out a thick wad of clippings. "Evelyn Caldwell to Star in *Night Magic.*" "Caldwell Wins Tony." "Evelyn Caldwell Filming in Greece." "Caldwell Nominated for Oscar."

"Oh, wow," Nancy said out loud, shaking her

head. One actress never quite becoming a star, the other soaring to the top. It was amazing that they had remained friends.

Or had they?

Marla was a talented actress. Was she performing now, pretending to like Evelyn? Was she really forgetful? Or was she the sharp poker player Nancy had seen in the kitchen a little while ago?

Was Marla here to help Evelyn with the Red Barn or destroy it?

Nancy replaced the album in the suitcase and instead of returning to the party walked slowly to her cabin. Only two things were certain: They'd made it through the night safely, and she still hadn't identified the arsonist.

The next day almost everyone slept in, enjoying their first day off in weeks. Breakfast was served late in the morning. During it, Evelyn made a surprise announcement. Charles Ferguson had called to invite them all over to his place for an afternoon of sledding.

"But, please, everyone, be careful," Evelyn concluded. "We have a performance tonight plus the rest of the run, and we don't have room for any more wheelchairs."

Everyone laughed, but Nancy was worried. Why would Ferguson ask them over? What was the motive behind this strange invitation?

While Evelyn gave the cast and crew notes on

the previous night's performance, Nancy warned the security guards she'd be away for a while.

Evelyn and George wanted to give the horses some exercise, so they rode them over to Ferguson's. The others went in cars, with Nancy driving Ned, Sherri, and Ben.

Ferguson appeared delighted to see them. A bonfire was blazing at the foot of a long, steep hill, and sleds and toboggans were lined up ready for action. The snow was thick and crunchy, the sky clear with a bright, cold sun overhead.

At first Nancy was watchful, studying both Marla and Ferguson, who had attached himself to Evelyn, taking runs on the toboggan with her. His gruffness was gone, replaced with the charming manner of a good host. Evelyn sparkled under his attention.

Marla joined in the spirit of the day, trudging up the hill pulling a sled and shouting with joy as she slid down. Hearing her hearty laugh, Nancy found it difficult to believe her suspicions from the night before. Just because Marla had a reason to be jealous of Evelyn didn't make her a criminal. Besides, she was the victim of the scaffold accident. If she had rigged that trap, she would never have gone up on the stage. She did, though, and came within an inch of being killed.

"Come on, Nancy." Ned held up a two-person sled. "Stop wearing your detective face. This baby has your name on it."

She couldn't resist his invitation. They took

several runs, then raced each other on single sleds. The crisp air, the clean sky, and the pleasure of whizzing down the snowy slope soon took over, pushing problems out of her mind. Between runs, hot chocolate warmed their cold noses and frozen fingers.

The sun was getting low in the sky when they once more climbed on the toboggan. Evelyn was up front with Ferguson behind her, followed by Nancy and Ned. Fiona gave them a push and they started down, gaining speed. Suddenly Sherri's sled cut in front of them. "Lean to the right!" Ned yelled.

It was too late. The toboggan hit the tail end of the sled and turned over. Nancy heard a yelp of pain.

When the riders unscrambled themselves, they found Evelyn bent over, holding her wrist. She was half laughing, half crying. "I told everyone to be careful. Why didn't *I* listen?"

Nancy gently checked her wrist. "I don't think it's too bad."

"I'm taking you to the emergency room," Charles announced.

They loaded her on the toboggan and eased her down the hill. As Charles helped her into his sports car, Evelyn said, "The horses. I forgot that I rode over here."

"Don't worry," Nancy said. "I'll ride Applause back."

George decided to take one last run while

Nancy went into the barn to saddle up. She was about to put the bridle on the mare when she sensed movement behind her. Before she could turn around, something cut into her throat, choking off her breath. An evil-smelling pad covered her mouth and nose.

Nancy struggled and twisted, trying to break free. She tried a sharp jab with her elbow and heard a slight "Umph," but the pressure on her neck didn't let up and dizziness overwhelmed her.

Points of light and darkness stabbed her eyes as she fought for air. Her body grew heavy . . . her knees gave way. She was falling . . . falling. . . .

Chapter Fifteen

NANCY WOKE UP SLOWLY, her head aching and her neck stiff. She had a terrible taste in her mouth. For a while she lay still, fighting nausea and dizziness. When she tried to open her eyes, she found they'd been taped shut. Her mouth was also taped and her wrists and ankles bound.

It was terribly cold. She began to wiggle around, partly to get her circulation going and partly to figure out where she was. She was in a small space with a low roof.

After a couple of minutes, her head began to clear and she realized her kidnapper had made a major mistake. Her hands were tied together in front, rather than behind her. She raised her arms and ripped at the tape on her eyes and mouth. Then with her teeth she pulled it off her wrists. Finally she freed her ankles.

Now she could identify her surroundings by touch, even though it was pitch-dark. She was lying on rough carpeting, surrounded by metal. Under the carpet she felt a tire, which confirmed her suspicions. She was in the trunk of a car.

She found the latch and tried to open the trunk, but it wouldn't budge. Feeling around in the blackness, she uncovered the car's jack. Using the handle as a lever, she pried at the latch until finally it popped.

Nancy climbed out and leaned against the fender for a moment, dizzy from the effort. The night sky and the dark woods were a welcome sight, and the cold fresh air helped drive away her nausea. She had no idea where she was, though.

She recognized the car—it was Evelyn's. But Evelyn hadn't driven it. She'd been taken to the hospital. Who, then? It could have been anyone. She remembered that Evelyn usually left the keys under the driver's seat.

Don't waste time worrying about that now, Nancy told herself. The luminous dial of her watch told her it was a half hour to curtain. Someone wanted her out of the way for a reason. He or she could be starting a fire in the Barn right now. She had to get back as fast as she could. She glanced around. Which way to go?

She spotted the moon reflecting off a glimmer of water in the distance. Stumbling over roots and vines, she made her way to the river and the path along it. Was the Barn downriver to her left or upriver to her right? Closing her eyes, she tried to visualize the area, as if looking at a map. She turned right, praying she had made the correct choice.

Half walking, half trotting, she moved along the slippery path as quickly as she could. The minutes dragged on forever. The path seemed endless. Finally she came upon the cabins. She didn't pause but ran straight ahead toward the Barn.

The lobby was empty except for a security guard. The doors to the theater were closed, and Howie was alone in the box office. He looked up in surprise. "What happened to you? We were all worried. Evelyn called the police."

"Tell you later. Is everything all right?" He and the security guard nodded. Nancy slipped through the door into the theater. The play had just begun, and she stood watching for a moment. All was normal.

She went out to check the rest of the Barn, to make sure there were no problems in the office or bathrooms.

She was headed outside to go around backstage when Marla came out of the theater into the lobby. The actress stopped dead in her tracks when she saw Nancy. Her mouth fell open in surprise. "What are *you* doing here? I—I mean, what happened? Where did you go? We've had the police looking for you."

"Someone kidnapped me." Nancy watched Marla closely for her reaction.

"Kidnapped? What do you mean?" The actress's face was very pale.

Nancy explained. Marla said nothing for a moment, then turned to the box office. "Howie, call the police and tell them she's back safe and sound." She studied Nancy. "You're rather a mess, aren't you?"

Nancy glanced down. The sleeve of her pink jacket was torn, probably snagged on a bush. Grease and dirt were smeared on her clothes. "I'll clean up later."

Instead she stood outside, watching the lobby through a window until she saw Marla pour a cup of coffee at the refreshment stand and go back into the theater. Had she come out to set another fire and changed her mind? She certainly had been very surprised to see Nancy.

Nancy waited a minute, then sneaked back inside and told the security guard to keep an eye on Marla. Then she walked around the Barn to the stage entrance.

Ned and George were overjoyed to see Nancy. Ned wrapped her in a warm hug. "We were so worried about you," he whispered. "We looked everywhere."

Nancy told them the story, then asked, "Who was missing after I disappeared?"

"Well, people began to leave after Evelyn was

hurt, but Joseph and Fiona helped us search for you," Ned said.

"Joseph!"

"Yeah, can you believe it?" George grinned. "He was really nice about it, too."

"What about Marla?" Nancy asked.

Ned frowned. "I don't remember seeing her."

"Neither do I," George said. "But—it couldn't be her, could it?"

"I don't want to believe it either, but she has just become my number-one suspect. Anyway, *someone* wanted me out of the way for a reason. Come on, we need to make a thorough check backstage." Nancy headed for Laura's dressing room. "Look for anything suspicious, anything that might start a fire."

They searched carefully but found nothing. When the first act ended, Nancy quietly checked the stage and set while the curtain was down, then hurried around front to keep an eye on Marla.

The actress stood calmly next to Evelyn, who was chatting with people during intermission, her arm in a sling. "It's nothing really, just a slight sprain," Evelyn said in answer to a man's question. As soon as she spotted Nancy, she excused herself and hurried over. "What happened? I'm so relieved to see you!"

"I'll explain later," Nancy said. "But don't worry, I'm fine."

Intermission and the second act passed without any problems. Nancy changed into clean clothes before joining the others in the Lodge after the play.

The second night's gathering was more subdued. Evelyn, Laura, and Matt all had important friends up from New York, and the young crew members were happy to be introduced to well-known theater folk. Music played softly while groups chatted and mingled.

Nancy was talking to a Broadway director and his wife when she noticed that Marla was gone. Excusing herself, she glanced around but didn't see either George or Ned. No time to waste, she thought, and hurried outside. A light was on in Marla's room. She ran to Evelyn's house and dashed upstairs. She was hoping against hope that the actress was simply tired and had left the party early.

Instead she found ashes in the bedroom fireplace. From the few charred scraps remaining, it was clear these were the clippings from the envelope in the back of the scrapbook. One scrap showed a picture of Evelyn's face, crossed out with angry slashes.

Nancy raced down the stairs and to the Barn. The front doors were locked, but the stage door creaked open when she turned the knob. The stage was lit by fluorescent work lights.

Marla was kneeling beside the lowered curtain,

heaping Laura's costumes in a pile. A can of lighter fluid stood next to her, and the usual cigarette was in her hand.

Nancy stepped quietly onto the stage. She was about fifteen feet away when the actress spotted her.

Marla screamed and jumped to her feet, grabbing the can of lighter fluid. "Stay right there! Don't move!"

"Give me the can, Marla." Nancy spoke calmly and quietly, as she would to a nervous horse.

Marla popped open the top of the can. "She's only getting what she deserves! It's time for her to lose it all, just like I did!"

"I know you lost your theater, and I know how Evelyn took over your part on Broadway." Nancy took a step, edging closer to Marla. "I understand why you're bitter, Marla, but burning down the Barn won't change the past."

"It will change her future!" Marla's laugh was thin and high-pitched. "She'll find out how it feels to lose everything you love! They took away my playhouse because it was losing money. Now I'm taking away hers."

She waved her arms wildly and cigarette ashes fell on the costumes.

Nancy knew she had to distract her. "You're so clever, Marla. That scaffold trap really fooled me. How could you be sure I'd pull you to safety in time?"

"Ha! You're the great Nancy Drew, aren't you?

If you failed and I was killed, well, so what? What do I have to live for? And if I was only hurt, I'd sue the socks off Evelyn and she'd be in debt for the rest of her life."

Nancy slowly slid one foot forward, then transferred her weight onto it. "Marla, you have a lot to live for. You're so talented and so clever. How did you manage to rig all those lines in the short time between the end of rehearsal and dinner?"

She puffed rapidly on her cigarette. "I knew what I was doing. It wasn't hard. Then I set the prop shed on fire to welcome you. All those lovely old scripts lying around just begging to start a fire."

"How did you ever manage to pull off that trick with the wrench?" Nancy had to keep her talking while she inched closer to the actress.

Marla smiled proudly. "Easy. I ran the fishing line to the back of the theater near the lobby door. I just had to slip inside for a second, give the line a yank, and cut it. Then I was back in the lobby, innocently working on the display."

"Did you push Matt off the path?"

Marla waved the open can and some fluid squirted out. "Of course not. Why would I want to hurt him? That was an accident."

"Why did you leave the note on my bed Tuesday night? That was risky. Someone could have seen you," Nancy said, taking a slow step forward.

"Not me—I was too careful. I just wanted to test you, to see if I could scare you off."

"You could have killed a lot of people in the theater last night if I hadn't put out that fire in the men's room," Nancy said evenly.

Marla waved her arms, splashing more liquid on the curtain, scattering cigarette ashes. She didn't seem to notice. "With the great Miss Drew and all those guards around? But I would have busted up the play and Evelyn wouldn't have had her big success." She laughed hysterically.

"How did you know where to find George and me when we were out riding the horses?" Nancy edged closer. A few more feet and she'd be able to tackle Marla.

"I cruised up and down the road, knowing you'd show up sooner or later."

"But Howie said you were in the office, setting up the press conference. He heard you through the door."

Marla laughed. "It was a snap. I taped some calls, then left them playing while I was gone."

"Clever, Marla. Very clever. Why did you pretend to be friends with Evelyn all these years?"

"She was a contact! She could have found parts for me in her films or plays. But she didn't! Not once! She's a fool!"

Nancy could tell Marla was out of control. She edged forward another step.

"Did you see the way I jerked her around with

those notes?" Marla went on. "The ninny fell for it every time. A puppet on a string, that's what she is. I pulled the string and she jumped. Did you see how eager she was to believe the note saying the danger was over? All she cared about was her infernal play."

"You really hate her, don't you?" Only a few feet to go, Nancy thought.

"Hate? That's too mild. Try *loathe, despise, detest.*" She spat out the words, then suddenly straightened up. "Stop right there, Miss Nosy Drew. Don't come any closer."

Marla grinned and squirted more liquid on the curtain and the pile of clothes. The sharp odor of the fluid filled the air.

Nancy made a leap for Marla and managed to grab her by the ankles. They crashed to the stage but Marla was quick and strong. She wiggled out of Nancy's grasp like a snake and threw herself on top of the girl, pinning her facedown on the pile of costumes.

The fluid's acrid odor filled Nancy's nose. Marla's knee pressed down on her spine. One hand grabbed her right arm, forcing it back against her shoulder blade.

"Where's that cigarette?" Marla grunted. "Ah, here it is."

She leaned over to grab the lit cigarette, which had rolled a few feet away. "Now, Miss Detective Drew, the Barn is going up in flames, just as I promised. And you're going to burn with it!"

Chapter Sixteen

WHEN MARLA REACHED for the cigarette, Nancy felt the actress's weight shift off the center of her back and the pressure on her arm lessen. Nancy drew up her knees, wrapped her free arm around the back of Marla's neck, and violently threw herself to the left, twisting her body and pulling Marla over with her as she rolled.

Marla roared with anger, and her cigarette dropped onto the pile of costumes. Laura's velvet dress burst into flames inches from them. Nancy had to ignore the fire while she struggled with the tall, wiry actress.

Using all her strength, Nancy managed to flip Marla over, pressing her facedown on the stage. She secured one arm in a hammerlock, then the other. The actress kicked and fought furiously, shouting and cursing, vowing to kill Nancy.

The flames grew, beginning to travel up the curtain. Nancy didn't dare let go of Marla and could only watch as the fire spread.

Over Marla's screams of rage, Nancy heard a door bang open.

"Nancy!" Ned shouted as he and George ran onto the stage. They took one look at the fire and spun around. "We'll get the extinguishers!"

"Hurry!" Nancy shouted.

They ran back seconds later, armed with one extinguisher each.

Nancy kept a tight grip on Marla, who bucked and heaved and yelled while Ned and George directed the foam at the flames.

George sprayed the pile of costumes, and Ned attacked the curtain. Fortunately the huge curtain was made of fire-resistant material, and once the lighter fluid had been consumed the flames died down. Eventually the fire went out.

George ran to call the police while Nancy stared at the charred curtain, blinking smoke-stung eyes.

Marla was finally quiet, and Ned helped her to her feet, keeping one arm pressed behind her back. It was only a precaution. All the fight had gone out of the actress. She collapsed on the couch and remained motionless until the police arrived.

* * *

It was after midnight by the time the police finished questioning them. They had found the security guard who had been assigned to the Barn that night. He was tied up in Matt's dressing room, unhurt but groggy from the ether that Marla had used to knock him out.

Marla had been taken away, looking frail and broken as she was guided into the squad car.

Now Nancy and her friends relaxed in Evelyn's living room, sipping steaming mugs of cocoa.

"I'm going to hire the best lawyer I can find for her," Evelyn said firmly. "I can hardly believe this has happened. Poor Marla is obviously emotionally ill. She doesn't belong in prison."

Nancy watched the lights twinkling on Evelyn's Christmas tree. "But she committed a crime."

Evelyn leaned forward. "From what you told me, the shock of losing her theater must have caused her to behave that way. I'll do everything I can to see that she gets proper treatment. I have to take care of her. She's my friend."

Nancy remembered the way Marla viciously spat out the words *loathe, despise, detest.*

"She's certainly a talented actress," George said. "Pretending to be so silly and forgetful, and all the while rigging those traps. She even had the sense to start a fire in the men's room instead of the ladies'."

"With the wastebasket so near the door," Ned

said, "we should have guessed that anyone could have tossed a cigarette into it."

Evelyn took a small sip from her mug. "I should have been suspicious when she arrived here, acting so absentminded. But it had been years since I'd seen her, and we all change over time."

"It was a clever disguise," Nancy said. "She could show up wherever she wanted with the excuse that she was searching for something."

"Marla's always been clever," Evelyn said. "We did summer stock together one year as apprentices. She could take on any job in the theater, from set design to box office to—"

"Rigging special effects?" Nancy asked.

"Yes. It's too bad I didn't remember that earlier." Evelyn's smile was sad.

"You had a lot on your mind," Nancy said gently.

Evelyn sighed. "Yes, the play. I was foolish not to listen to you, Nancy. You could have been killed tonight."

"I'm good at investigating crimes, and you're good at producing and directing hit plays." Nancy paused. "What will happen with *Alias Angel Divine?* Will you be able to continue the run?"

"Yes, just as soon as we can replace Laura's costumes and the curtain, and clean up the smoke damage. I hope to reopen in a few days."

Nancy stood up and walked to the window. "Between the repairs and the tickets you'll have to refund, it's going to be costly."

"I'm not too worried about finances now." Evelyn leaned back against the couch. "After the performance tonight, two more people offered to back a Broadway production, and Joseph's had an offer for the film rights."

"You mean it's going to be made into a movie?" George asked. "That's great, Aunt Evelyn!"

"Nothing is definite until the contracts are signed, but Broadway, at least, is certain now." She winked at George. "I didn't tell you yet, but I picked up another angel this afternoon."

"Who?" George looked puzzled.

"Our friendly neighbor, Charles Ferguson."

"You're kidding!" Ned said.

"And he also seems to be, um—interested in pursuing a . . . relationship." She blushed slightly.

"What?" George said.

Evelyn held up her hand, stopping her. "He's really not so bad. That crusty act he puts on covers his soft spots. Inside he's rather a sweetheart."

Nancy was as surprised as the others. "So that's why he invited us sledding."

Evelyn nodded. "I've had a lot of men fall for me in the past, but he really took me by surprise."

George leaned over and hugged her. "I'm happy for you, Aunt Evelyn."

Later Nancy, Ned, and George headed down the path toward their cabins. They'd be going home the next day.

Nancy linked arms with her two friends. "How did you guys know to come to the Red Barn?"

"It was funny," George said. "I was talking to Matt and suddenly saw Ned. At that same moment he noticed me. We both realized you were gone, and we just knew you were in trouble."

"I said, 'Nancy,' and George said, 'Let's go.' We didn't waste any time getting over there." Ned kissed the top of Nancy's head.

"Thank goodness for that." Nancy sighed. "I sure was glad to see you two."

"Hey, what are friends for?" George's laugh rang out in the crisp night air.

"I guess it will be hard to say goodbye to Matt tomorrow, won't it?" Nancy said.

"Yes. He said he'd call or write, but I don't know if he means it. Even if I never see him again, it's been wonderful. Besides, Bess is going to just die when she finds out I've spent all this time with Brent of 'Ventura Boulevard.'"

"She sure will." Nancy squeezed Ned's arm. "What about you, Ned? Are you going to miss Laura?"

"Yeah, a lot."

"What?" Nancy stopped to stare up at him.

He smiled. "Get real, Drew." He kissed her cheek. "It's flattering to have a beautiful actress fall all over you. But I like my women strong and independent—just like someone I happen to know."

Nancy's next case:

Supermodel Martika Sawyer has invited Nancy Drew to the grand opening of Cloud Nine—her health spa and resort on a private Caribbean island. But there's serious trouble in the tropical paradise. A fantasy world of blue skies, white sands, and emerald waters, Cloud Nine has suddenly come under siege, its future threatened by a tidal wave of crime.

Martika's guest list sparkles with celebrities: famous financiers, champion athletes, movie stars. But beneath the glitter lurks a shocking secret and a twisted plot. Nancy's investigation into the conspiracy leads her into a web of jealousy, greed, and deception in which the ultimate intrigue is murder . . . in *If Looks Could Kill*, Case #91 in The Nancy Drew Files™.